# ELEMENTS

## An Anthology

# ELEMENTS

## An Anthology

Presented by
**Dublin Creative Writers**
*Dublin, Ohio*

Published by
**SPARKSTREET MEDIA, LLC**
HTTP://WWW.SPARKSTREETMEDIA.COM/

PO Box 3155
Dublin, Ohio 43016

## ELEMENTS: An Anthology
Presented by Dublin Creative Writers
Dublin, Ohio

Cover Design & Illustration
Copyright © 2024 Olga Begak

Curated and edited by:
Sara Elliott
Anita Howitt
Val George

Copyedited by
J. Powell Ogden
Jeanette Ogden
Maddie Ogden

Interior Design and Formatting by We Got You Covered Book Design
WWW.WEGOTYOUCOVEREDBOOKDESIGN.COM

Paperback ISBN: 978-1-7376609-7-2
Ebook ISBN: 978-1-7376609-6-5

# ACKNOWLEDGMENTS

*Sara Elliott, Anita Howitt, Val George, Marília Bonelli, Kristen Whitney,* and the whole team at Dublin Creative Writers would like to extend a heartfelt thank you to our fabulous Kickstarter backers who made this anthology possible, including:

Alexandra Corrsin, Amy A Gordon, Andrea Watson, Autumn Shah, az_sardog, Belinda Kroll, Boris Veytsman, Brian Nutwell, David Hoffman, Eron Wyngarde, Jenn G, Kevin L. Powers, Kristen Whitney, Lauren Prettyman-Brown, Marília Bonelli, Mary Jo Rabe, Memmie, Molly, Ray Pantle, Robert M. Nutwell, Roxane Llanque, Ruth Ann Orlansky, Sam Driscoll, Sarah McHatton, Sheryl Parbhoo, Shruti Gupta, Sirrah Medeiros, Tara Stayton.

# TABLE OF CONTENTS

"The sky broke like an egg into full sunset and the water caught fire."

Pamela Hansford Johnson

DUBLIN CREATIVE WRITERS
of Dublin, Ohio


# PRESENTS


Since time immemorial, literature has consistently drawn from the natural world for inspiration. Working with elements like earth, wind, fire, water, and aether/spirit, twenty featured writers from around the world explore our natural environment through the lens of fiction. In this vastly diverse collection of micro-fiction, flash fiction and short stories that span a broad spectrum of genres, nature is not just a resource to be protected or exploited, but rather a generative force with its own sentient power.

Mining the elements both as material and metaphor, the contributing authors treat nature as a model for negotiating the complexities of modern life. Informed by an elemental logic, their stories envision new ways we might relate to the natural world and to one another.

**Dublin Creative Writers** presents our fifth collection, *Elements, An Anthology.* Conceived during a time when climate crisis, anthropogenic disasters and their inescapable intersection with issues of equality and social justice, this collection strives not only to entertain but to offer new ways of thinking about the elements beyond the registers of conventional discourse.

We hope you enjoy reading these original works as much as we enjoyed curating them for you. May they inspire you, enlighten you, and provide you with an opportunity to tap into the spirit of innovation and resilience that lives within us all.

**SARA ELLIOTT**
**ANITA HOWITT**
**VAL GEORGE**
Editorial Board
November 2024

# BUT THEY SING GLORIOUSLY

## By R. A. O'Brien

THE FIRST BABY BORN with nubbins arrived on 7th November at 10:03 p.m. in a small hospital in a country town in the West Australian wheat belt. Think: open land rolling away to the horizon, straw-colored wheat-stubble, grazing, grubby-fleeced sheep, and the smell of eucalypts and dust. The town population was 1,477 + 1. Tiny. Blink and you'd miss it. The town and the hospital both. The baby, too. Tiny and very sweet. But.

The midwife and doctor both thought the newborn's bone structure looked odd, not quite right—the shoulder blades were malformed and the arm bones seemed particularly long. They sent the mother and the baby—a girl called Marjorie—to a bigger hospital. Better facilities. Medical specialists. The doctor and midwife in the country town washed their hands of it. Went home, ate, went to bed. Not together, although she wouldn't have minded, but the doctor hadn't figured that out. Tomorrow would be another day.

As happens, tomorrow faded past as well. A few days after that there was a piece in the newspaper. Then they remembered.

By the time the newspaper caught wind of the story, seven babies with nubbins on their shoulder blades had been born throughout the wheat belt. Because the big smoke was Perth, and because there was only one hospital there specializing in maternal and infant health, the babies all ended up in the same place. A funnel effect. If the nubbins had started somewhere else—in Europe or the US or South America or someplace— it might have taken much longer to piece things together. But the wheat belt is close to empty and the structure of the health system created an agglomeration of strangeness. Peculiar babies became visible quickly. The public health apparatus swung into action. The well-being of the infants was closely monitored.

The newspaper piece was written simply to fill up the pages. Summer. Shortly after Christmas. And no bushfires to report. They would surely come, but not yet. A slow news week. The paper had needed to find local interest stories. Otherwise, the story might never have seen the light of day.

Its first appearance was on page twelve. A long way in from the front and an even number. People look at the odd-numbered pages first. Sometimes they miss looking at the even-numbered ones altogether. A page twelve human-interest story. Ho-hum.

The TV stations were just as news-deprived and one of them tumbled to the idea of running the baby story. It wouldn't really be a repeat; they had the advantage of cameras. The other nine babies (now a total of ten) were sick, asleep, or crying, but Marjorie 'gooed' and smiled and didn't cry a bit. The news crew took hours of video.

Marjorie was a particularly endearing newborn. She had a fine-featured face, long, slender arms and fingers, a pretty mop of curly black hair, and wide-awake eyes. The nubbins on her shoulder blades were visible, even in the footage—no small thing given the crew was not permitted to set up lights in the hospital and the camera tended to make everything look flatter than it was. Instant poster-child.

The slow summer news continued. Cricket. Heat waves. Crowds at the beach. Sticky ice-creams. Sand so hot it burned your feet.

*Got a beer in that cooler?*

*Put some sunscreen on.*

*Want to come over on Sunday for a barbie?*

*Didja see the story about the babies? It was on the news last night.*

*Yeah, pretty kid, but weird to have so many, eh?*

The lack of news created opportunities. A loose coalition developed. Green-ish influencers, lobby groups (some solid, some mad as cut snakes), political parties looking for airtime, members of Parliament, sensationalists, believers in alien abductions, concerned parents, PC academic humanists, intrigued medical researchers, anti-vaxxers, and a group calling itself the Alliance Against Coal-Fired Electricity Plants (AACFEP), all shared a concern about the babies' welfare. Strangest of all, a group of citizens worried about the discharge of bilge water into the local marine environment also took up the babies' cause. Everybody wanted exposure. The most popular hashtag in the relevant part of the cyberverse was initially *#BabyDeformities*, then

*#BabyModifications*, then, finally, *#BabyMods*. Most thought the baby mods were the result of pollution. Blamed toxic farming methods, petrochemical aerosol sprays, GM foods, ground water. Blamed God (some did, privately). Blamed science. Blamed greed.

As well as their structural oddities, at birth the babies were covered in a colorless, fine, downy hair. By three months the hair had disappeared, then the feathers started appearing. At first, only a tuft poked through the nubbins' skin, skin that seemed itchy. The babes wriggled endlessly, seemingly to scratch their backs. X-rays, MRIs, blood tests. Nothing conclusive except conclusive oddness. By week 14 there were 79 babies born with nubbins, 31 of whom were showing feathers. By week 27 the number of baby mod cases had risen to 113. Most had feathers. No new baby mod cases had come to light for five weeks. It seemed as if the avalanche of new strange kids might have slowed and the total number of occurrences peaked. That was the point at which the feathered nubbins began to stretch and open, to unfurl.

The hospital staff tried to keep knowledge of the wings under wraps, tried to give the infants and their parents some privacy. Might as well have tried to stop the planet spinning on its axis.

Medical specialists were deeply divided. Some wanted to amputate the wings immediately, arguing that doing so would give the babies the best chance of a normal life. Some argued that the functionality of the wings had yet to be established, so why assume they'd be a bad thing? Others argued that parents had a right to choose, if they wished, to have their infant's wings 'surgically adjusted'.

Meanwhile, the news leaked. Someone called them 'angels' and it stuck. The reporters had a label. The public's imagination was hooked. The supernatural was now definitely in play.

The cathedral priests met at breakfast.

One said to the other, "Did you see the page three photo?"

A raised eyebrow.

"I didn't think they did that sort of thing in this newspaper."

The paper was picked up, the page turned.

"Damn. We'll have to let his nibs know."

As they anticipated, the archbishop was less than impressed.

"Angels. For God's sake. No one except the ignorant and superstitious believe in angels anymore. The Second Vatican Council should have done something useful and ruled them out. Well, we've lost that opportunity. Bloody nonsense."

The Catholic archbishop conferred with his Anglican counterpart.

"Visitations of the Virgin and appearances of saints are quite problematic enough. We don't need angels. These fantasies always give rise to fallacies amongst the faithful."

"I agree," said the Anglican counterpart. "They lead the people astray from obedience to the church."

The Catholic archbishop looked meaningfully across the desk. "And they're bad press. Look at the trouble we had last time the Virgin appeared. Complaints from government. Religious tourism running out of control. Thousands of people camping out. It was a mess."

"We certainly wouldn't be acting responsibly if we didn't protect our congregations from unscrupulous scammers, liars, and fake news," the Anglican counterpart said, smiling.

So, they were in communion. For once. Not that it made any difference.

The babies' wings grew. An entranced public watched it all on YouTube. Especially Marjorie. She was still poster-child #1. Her father never said no to a camera. By the time the children were eighteen months of age, there were signs that their wings would eventually be able to hold them aloft. Learning to fly seemed as innate as learning to walk. Like fledgling birds, they flapped their wings endlessly. As they grew stronger, they practiced tiny lift-offs. Fell short distances. Maneuvered to gain directional control. Rehearsed landings.

Walking, flying, talking, running. Finding a ball and throwing it. Patting the family dog. Delivering big smackeroo kisses. Waving goodbye. The babies, now toddlers, were learning it all.

The press started to call the parents 'philangeli', friends of angels. Tourist companies organized pilgrimages taking the gawking credulous from home to home, driving down the streets on which the philangeli lived, all on the off chance of seeing a winged child. Some of the philangeli put out nails to puncture the tires of the curious. Others put out collection boxes. Many moved house, changed their names.

Then someone had the bright idea of doing a genetic analysis. Check that the kids were from the right parents, hatched in the appropriate place, not from the wrong nest. Not cuckoos. And— surprise, surprise—there in the genetic code, was an anomaly. A sequence inserted that shouldn't have been there. An ornithological snip, slidden into their human code. But by what means? When they were born, the angels had been far flung, strewn over an area larger than England. There were those who said the mothers had been fucking emus, or that they had been abducted by aliens-with-plumage and implanted with rogue DNA. It remained a mystery, and about that mystery no one with a claim to relevant expertise expressed any opinion whatsoever.

By the time the children were around five years old they flew well and had started school. They were robust and healthy, they walked and talked and wanted their parents to read them bedtime stories. They liked or hated school lunch boxes, swimming and ballet lessons, drawing, arithmetic, hopscotch, video games, being alone, being at the center of a crowd, birthday parties, burgers, dogs, cats, horses, the color yellow, and a million other things. Apart from the wings, they were normal children. Well, the wings and one other thing: they could all sing.

Under the supervision of her parents, Marjorie continued to be the poster-child for the angels. Cute as a button and such pretty wings. She smiled willingly for the cameras. Besides, she was the forerunner of all that came. Her father thought she was the bee's knees, wings and all. Her mother wasn't so sure—she was already frightened before the Molotov cocktail shattered their bedroom window late one Friday night.

Marjorie was hurt in the ensuing blaze. One wing was burned badly, feathers seared off. What remained turned from white to black. The medicos thought they might have to amputate but decided to try saving the wing. They didn't know if she would fly again. Didn't know who they could call upon to help with her rehabilitation. In the end, they called in the people who dealt with injured raptors, got them to help with her retraining and physiotherapy. Slowly, she recovered. But she was fearful, jittery. She was no longer the same Marjorie. Her mother wasn't the same, either. Scoured by media attention and violence, she'd had enough. She wouldn't be Marjorie's mummy anymore.

The homeless man who prowled the botanic gardens near the opera house in Sydney changed his sign. *Repent for the Kingdom of Heaven is nigh* was discarded. The new sign read: *Some have entertained angels unawares.* In Melbourne, someone had started writing *Angels* in empty spaces on buildings, footpaths, steps, river embankments. A beautiful cursive script in glowing, golden chalk. There was talk of a new Australian movie being made—the working title was *Strangers*.

So, there we were—media, citizens, politicians, churches, and all—alone with the possibility of having to welcome something completely new amongst us. An unhappy prospect.

Canberra was busy, Parliament was sitting. "It won't do, Minister," Max said. He was wearing his particularly proper minister's adviser face.

"What do you expect me to do, Max? They're children, for God's sake. How would it look if I had them bumped off or imprisoned?"

"They are not children, they're aberrations. Things that should never have been born."

"I've seen the photos. They look quite attractive. What's all this shite about?"

"They're birds, Minister."

"Don't be idiotic."

"Feathers, thus birds."

"Feathers, thus angels. I've seen those twee Christmas cards with Raphael's cherubs on them. So have half the population. No, Max. We wouldn't be able to sell that. Birds! No parent would buy it. Besides, I'd have to have new legislation. And before you go there, it isn't going to happen. Find something else to feed the press, can't you? A dash of some new hysteria should do it."

The minister's adviser drew a breath. "There are also financial implications."

"And what are those?"

"The scientists want special funds made available to study them. The medicos are claiming they need new Medicare-funded codes—higher rates—because they have to work harder and it takes more time to sort out ... whatever it is they sort out when one of these ... is brought in by its parents because it's sick. The clothing industry is in an uproar."

"Clothing? The rag trade?"

"Yes, they'll have to design new patterns for everything. It will cost them, Minister."

"Pardon me, but don't they develop new patterns for everything each season? I thought that was the whole point?"

"And they cost schools more. Can't sit on chairs, you see. Wings get in the way. They need stools."

"Look, Max, cut the crap. Something's got your knickers in a knot, and it's not stools or patterns."

"There's a new paper coming out. CSIRO and some university have done the research. They sent us a copy ahead of publication. Probably thought we'd give them an elephant stamp or something." Max paused.

"Don't keep me in suspense."

"There are too many people involved to suppress it."

The minister spoke in his quietest voice. His most dangerous one. "Why, exactly, would we want to suppress it?"

"They did some—I don't know. A genetic study plus some sort of anatomical thing. They can probably cross-breed. With us. You know, daughter marries thing-with-wings and Mum and Dad end up grandparents to an ornithological freak. It's one thing when it's someone else's kid and there's only a handful of them, then it's just weird. When they start invading your own family, though. Horrifying. Terrifying. The punters will never vote for it."

"It'll be a while before they hit puberty. We've got time."

"Two elections are all you can safely bet on, Minister."

The minister peered at his adviser over the edge of his glass of cabernet then carefully placed it down on the table. "I'll talk to the PM."

The angels seem comfortable enough in the enormous aviary

built for them at the zoo—government funded, of course. At first, they wept for their parents. Marjorie, especially, cried for her dad, her blackened wing trembling.

The sign on the cage reads: *Do not feed.* The unspecified nature of the occupants is a compromise. No one will approve *Do not feed the children* and mention of angels is verboten. Their meals are controlled. They don't seem to notice the contraceptives added to the food.

Someone has daubed writing on the concrete wall at the end of their cage. The paint is the same golden color as the chalk inscriptions. Whatever was written, it's mostly illegible now.

They spend their days in the heights. They rarely speak to passers-by and ignore their keepers. They have abandoned us. But they still sing gloriously.

# THE GODDESS OF KARRARA
## By Kelly Matsuura

FROM A YOUNG AGE, magick burned within my hands, aching to heal and create. But I was arrogant and impatient. I ignored the rules. I never feared the consequences.

Am I a god? No, I am flesh and blood, as are all my kin. I am a fire mage of the old Delta clan, people of the fire mountain and ash skies. When the mountain is restless, so are we. When it hungers, we are empty inside until satiation comes.

You asked me earlier for a story. Well, I have many stories; I have lived many long years in this world. I will tell you one now while you're resting, but you must let me tell it in my own way.

As a child, I had few friends. My mother kept me isolated, insisting my powers would develop further if away from other children. It was important to connect to the land and all nature, she said. To control my fire, I had to be one with it. I learned to walk on the burning coals and hold a steady flame in my open palms.

I enjoyed Mother's lessons and my growing skills, yet I was

lonely. One day, while practicing a fire spell of Mother's, my mind wandered, and I pictured a small brown bear like one I had seen a few times by the river. I layered words from the old spell with new ideas and called for that bear to be my friend. To my surprise and joy, I awoke from my trance-like state to witness the first fire-shifter of my creation. There was the young bear I had admired, seated back on his hind legs and licking one paw. Its form flickered from solid, natural, to the swirling curls of yellow flames that were distinctive of my clan's magick.

The bear turned my way and held my gaze. I admired the way fire rippled along its fur, across its back and down its legs, and how the tiniest of flames outlined the bear's black coal eyes. It opened its mouth and shot a flame my way, but I felt no threat from the creature. He was showing off for me.

I walked to him and stroked the top of his head. He responded with the sweetest sound, a cross between a low growl and the purr of a wild cat. He was mine. I laughed then, with my head thrown back, my hair blowing in the wind, and my voice echoing through the forest. I had magick like no other. I could make beasts! Living creatures sprung from my own imagination.

I would not give up the spell to anyone. This led to months of arguments with Mother, but she eventually let it go.

That all happened a long time ago, however. It was the true beginning, the time when I made the first fire-shifter. But yes, I know that's not what you want to know. You are only interested in how I made the Destroyer.

That is a difficult tale to share, even now.

No one ever figured out that I had the power to make such a man. People were so fooled, willing to believe any person of magick who claimed to be the creator. I kept my distance from it all and gave up seeing my old fire-shifter familiars for many years—to protect them.

All right, I'll tell you everything. But only because I'm old and the secret will remain between us. Also, I believe you are the only one strong enough to destroy the Man of Fire once and for all.

The fire-bear was unintentional; simply willed and sparked to life by my desire for a friend. But the fire-life spell worked over and over; virtually any animal I wanted to make, I could. The fire-shifters were always young though, I assume, because when I made the first one, I specifically wanted a baby bear. However, they would all grow to full size quickly and all behaved as expected for the type of animal they were. I did make a few crossbreeds, but they didn't survive long.

Ok, I'm getting to the man now. Don't rush me; it isn't easy to retrace one's fateful steps.

Back then I ran a market stall, selling tonics and simple potions to the village folk. I never took the fire-shifters there; only the members of my clan even knew they existed.

One day, a lady in mourning clothes approached me and asked if I could communicate with the dead. I told her no; I was a fire-witch and had no connection to the underworld. I recommended a few witches, but the woman shook her head. No, they weren't right for what she wanted.

She thanked me for the advice and handed me an envelope.

She then disappeared into the crowd, and I lost sight of her. New customers approached, and I forgot about the envelope until I was home that evening.

I opened it, expecting a small cash gift, but all it contained was a photograph of a man in fine gentleman's robes. Her husband, I had to assume. It was such an odd thing; I had no clue why she had left it with me. I did keep it in my purse for a few weeks on the chance she returned to the markets to explain, but I didn't see her again until many months later.

I was strangely drawn to the photograph. I looked at his face several times a day, wondering what his name was, what his voice had sounded like, and whether he had been a kind man. He was quite stiff and posed in the picture, but had good features and smooth, thick hair. Handsome.

After about a month of this, I grew tired of the situation. Thoughts of the man and the image of his face burned in my mind and distracted me from more important things. On impulse one night, I tossed the photograph into the cooking fire and recited a few words of a resting spell for the dead. I hadn't known the man, and I doubted my words reached him, but it felt right at the time.

What I didn't know, however, was that the photograph itself was already spelled—to link the image of the man to a witch capable of bringing him to life again. And that was all I could think about from that moment onwards. I became utterly obsessed with him—still not knowing his name—to the point where I could think of no one else and could never have a restful sleep.

No, no, it wasn't a love spell. He belonged to Radya; I was

simply chosen to burn for his physical presence in the world because of my talent for making fire-creatures.

Radya? Forgive me, yes, she was the woman in mourning. She also did the linking spell herself, as it turned out. She wasn't powerful at magick, nowhere near my capability, but she was creative with the little magick she could access. As angry as I was that she had involved me so deceitfully, I had to admire her cunning in the matter.

Back to the man. I fought off the longing for several weeks, trying to reverse the linking spell too, but had no success. I started seeing him around me, like a ghost. He wasn't there, but he wouldn't disappear either. He never spoke. How I ached to hear his voice in the room, to know what he sounded like and enjoyed talking about.

I was spelled to want this, you understand, yet was fully aware that it wasn't my true desire. Still, when you are stuck in a spell, it is so intrusive and controlling that there's nothing to be done. In the end, I rationalized that she was just a lonely, mediocre witch wanting her husband back beside her. Her spell didn't seem dangerous by any means. I envisioned making the fire-version of him and taking him to her, then I'd be done with them both.

Well, of course, I was foolish! Go to any village in this realm, and they have witnessed the Destroyer's wrath. He wasn't like the animals I created—they were all new spirits and peaceful. Even the carnivores were placid, having no need to eat real food. They all existed to be loyal companions and had no desires of their own.

The man should have been the same, just a flamed physical

replica of the husband Radya couldn't forget. He wasn't supposed to have a real personality at all. But someone or *something* came from the spirit world when I did the fire-life spell. Something never seen before in this world.

Yes, he was born a child, just like the animals. I tracked down Radya in Foxglove Valley and took him to her. She was overjoyed and not upset in the least when I drained the little magick she had remaining. I stayed a short time, and she told me a little about her husband. His name was Dinaf, or was it Dinall? I'm not sure now. It was a long time ago.

Anyway, I left, satisfied. The linking spell was gone, and I looked forward to being myself again. I did wonder how long it would take for the man to grow full-size, or even if he ever would. He was my first fire-person, and I had warned Radya he might not survive long.

You know a lot of this next part: how the fire-man grew with a hunger for human flesh. He would enter a village just as the sun rose, and every hut would be burned to the ground by nightfall. The poor villagers would then be found, mere bones and ash. Surviving witnesses saw him eating people as they screamed from the flames. He was ruthless and indiscriminate.

Word spread quickly of this demon. The devil himself, they said. As soon as I heard, I packed a bag and came to talk with two teenagers who had managed to flee and find safety. Karrara is one of the last communities in this region with castle walls; it was not surprising that so many people sought shelter here.

I told no one that I made the creature. Instead, I offered my aid in locating him and thought it would be a simple matter to kill him. Unfortunately, he and I had a connection. I could find the direction he had walked, but then he knew I was following him, and I could not gain on him. I could also not get close enough to set any kind of holding spell on him either. Finding myself at a dead end, I returned to Radya's house. There, at least, I thought I could learn more about her husband and if there was any cause for his violence to be understood.

She was a pile of bones, too. His first victim, most likely. Her death proved to me that the man had only her husband's face, but there was no trace of his soul in the creature.

What's that, dear? Yes, I did say you might be able to stop him, but that is a discussion for another day. When you are stronger. You really should sleep now.

All right, one last question.

The Destroyer disappeared for a few years. Even I lost connection with him. I knew he was still alive out there somewhere, though. A creature like that would not be killed easily, and if another witch had succeeded in ending him, I would have felt it. That's just how magick works.

So, many common people went back to their villages and normal lives, but I could never let my guard slip. I knew he'd return when he was hungry. When he finally did, more people died; however, there were more survivors because they knew what he was and what he could do. They were faster to react and take their families to safety.

He's still out there. Hunting. He can't breach the Karrara's castle walls, so don't be afraid. You are safe, protected by the wall, the guards, and my magick shields.

Sleep now. You need more time. I'll be back when you are at full strength.

Good, you're awake. You slept for so many days this time, I wasn't sure you would ever stop growing.

Let me look at you. Perfect! My greatest creation yet. Every muscle strong, your eyes hold firm determination. You *will* dominate him. He will not see your power until it's too late.

Your name is Lora. I'm sorry it took so long for me to choose it. Your name was drawn from the source magick I used in your creation spell. A strong earth name.

You see, I realized the error I made in creating the man. I focused only on his image, making a half-person, an empty body for a demon to possess. You are a hybrid of magick—not pure fire like him and my animals, but a blend of fire and earth. The cost was high to work with the earth mages. They would not help me for naught, but in the end we all want the demon destroyed. I will pay what I must for being his creator.

It's time to take you outside and set you on your path. Come with me now and stay close to my side. Don't mind the stares of the locals. You are a great wonder to them—something they don't understand but have put all their faith in. They will worship you for centuries to come.

Ah, you like the world? The sunshine? It *is* marvelous. I love this land, perhaps more than my home. Here, the mountains touch the heavens, and the forests are so green—like dark jade. The waters around here are naturally healing and divine, the best in all these lands.

Mind your step here. We'll first go up to the parapet so I can show you the outside land and the path you must follow. I'm confident you won't need much direction though. Once you leave the castle walls, you will feel him, and he, you. He will head this way, and you will go to join him.

Do you understand your purpose now? Your life is bound to his, but you have the extra earth magick inside. It will devour you both at the moment of connection. His fire will live no more.

I hope you will be born again somewhere. Perhaps with the earth fae, they showed great interest in you at your infant stage. I hope they will protect you in a way I never can.

Do not call me Mother. I've never done anything to earn that right. Even my beautiful fire animals don't call me that.

Are you ready? I'll say goodbye to you from here. I want to stay here on the parapet and watch your journey. Enjoy the walk; every step you take in this world. I'm sorry you will only live a few days. Know that you will save this land and every living creature in it.

Join the Destroyer and save us. Please, Lora. Right my terrible wrong and be the great goddess this land has prayed for.

It is done. I know you can't hear me talking to you now, you are returned to dust, but I feel some comfort saying these last words to you as I kneel at your shrine.

Many others kneel with me.

Everyone in Karrara rushed to the lookouts and parapets to view the incredible orange fire miles in the distance. We knew what it was, but only I felt the magick drain from you, him, and me. I screamed in agony alongside the two of you, though no flames touched my skin. I fell to the ground, the connection lost; my magick, gone forever. At long last, it was done.

I think you called me 'Mother' again, or was I delusional? I don't deserve anyone's respect or love, but if you did call for me in your final seconds, it is a gift I would hold onto.

Your shrine is a work of delightful beauty and craftsmanship. I don't know the local artist's name, but he is a gifted young man who clearly fell in love with you in the seconds you passed him on the castle stairs that day. His love for you shines in every curve and groove in the stone he carved in your image. It is a true likeness and will stand long after all of us are gone and a new generation is left to care for this place.

Lora, Great Goddess of Karrara, Savior of Fire, and I'll say this now only because I'm sure you can't hear it—my daughter. Thank you for your sacrifice. You are divine.

# BAHIA
## By A.R. McHugh

BAHIA STANDS AT THE kitchen window and wonders why journalists' questions never change. *What's the last thing you remember? What did you think about as you bobbed about in the water, holding onto a piece of fuselage? Did you try to give up? Why do you think you alone were spared?*

She fills the kettle and looks out at patchy grass showing through the brown snow. Maybe she's wrong. There are some new questions. *Has it changed you? Do you still dream about it?* She returns to the woman in the living room while the kettle boils.

She works in a bank now, she says. She looks after her father and her siblings. She misses her mother. No, she has not flown since. No, she is not afraid to. No, it has not made her any more religious. It has not given her a mission. Sadly.

Shuttling back into the little kitchen, she makes a plunger of coffee and stays for a minute at the sink. Sometimes, she dreams that she is back in the dark sea, rocking and lapping among the bodies. The rock-slop-rock-slop thick taste of salt water, the smell of burning fuel, and large metal things bumping her are the obverse of every experience: getting on the bus, at the shops, sitting behind her plexiglass window at work, in the park with her father and nieces. At least she has no falling dreams. Instead of those, she wonders if her mother and the others were awake as they fell, seat-belted and tray-table-stowed, into the ocean.

This is the last interview, she thinks. No one will bother about the twentieth anniversary. She carries the coffee through on a tray with some biscuits. *So, has it changed you?* the woman asks.

Bahia wonders what headlines would look like if they were honest. News is how we distract ourselves from truths that we hope will not dawn on us until the end.

She does not like wide stretches of open sky – or water, but that's hardly a problem in Évry. She even gets out of the scarred family bathtub when the water is still warm. Once, she tried to stay in the scented steaming silence, but she began to smell the salt water of the Mozambique Channel, burning oil, the urine and vomit on the dead passengers bobbing around her, and got out. On Tuesdays, Thursdays, and Fridays, she handles business deposits in a windowless back office of the BNP Paribas Évry-Courcouronnes, and blesses the wall of spreadsheets between her and the memory of dawn on a limitless ocean, thirteen hours of dark water and heavy swell, and the intimate knowledge of fuselage buoyancy.

In an immeasurable moment in the watery dark, Bahia saw another figure clinging to the other side of the ragged panel, also half-collapsed over the torn avionic membrane. She wanted to slip beneath the salty chop, down, down, down where there was no light or time.

Dawn came with boats and hands and the dreadful haul and cold and questions without answers or end. Who do you think was rescued that night? Bahia thinks to the journalist on her sofa. My mother's child died in the rough dark sea; what lived was a blind incessant impulse without knowledge that kept kicking like a thing moved by an engine. Ignorance of this is the necessary trick of living, like ignoring the nose, which is constantly part of your vision.

*Has it changed you?*

Pressing lightly down on the plunger, she says, "I expect so."

# THE FOUNTAIN OF THE DANCING WINDS
## By LL Garland

"HOW IS IT A town this size does not have a witch?" Mayor Liviano stabbed the slab of cake in front of him with his fork. "Unheard of. Impossible," grumbled various members of the Council of Business. "How, indeed?"

"Maybe we don't need a witch, but rather a strong attraction to lure the people in. Here's one," The Magistrate, don Fisgón, picked up a brochure from the heap at the center of the table. *"Visit The Temple of the Dying Barbarians."* He swept off several cake crumbs and began to read, *"'How does a barbarian go about dying, you may ask. In the Age of Fire, the uncultured hordes of Remermark would go a-barbarianing, encountering myriad customs and cultures. Upon returning, many beat their swords into dye pots. With customary warlike passion, the barbarians recreated the vibrant colors and rich patterns they'd pillaged. Only this time without the bloodstains.'... Textiles? This is absolute garbage."*

"Perhaps, but that shabby dye shop was bursting at the seams with tourists itching to buy ugly bits of fabric. It was the same everywhere we visited," said señor Avaro, the Merchant. He fiddled with his pearl cufflinks, the finest Ysleta, Island of the Singing Scales, had to offer.

"But all these others—The Valley of Sneering Plague, City of the Flinching Streets, The

Pond of Swanning Obsidian... every single one was caused by a witch's curse. If we can't find a witch to curse us... we're doomed."

"You wouldn't believe the crowds in the City of Flinching Streets. Everywhere, gawking tourists and overflowing tills." The Merchant's palms started to itch.

"What about the Whispering Wood? Maybe that could be some sort of lure for tourists. We could play up the old tales. Have people dress up pretending to be magical forest creatures and jump out at the visitors. People pay decent money for that sort of nonsense, don't they?" the Magistrate suggested.

"If we cut away some of the trees we could add a few shops. Perhaps an inn or a theater. Maybe a train... We'd have to do something about the wind up there though. It's been getting worse lately. Can't have tourists getting hurt," added the Mayor.

"Good luck getting anything done as long as old what's-her-name's still there. Y'know, the hermit... Milagreta, up near Molino's Spire," huffed the Merchant. "Come to think of it, if you're looking for a witch, you can't do worse than her."

"That awful old woman who always has her dress on backwards?" asked the Mayor. "She's in here at least once a week, ranting at me, something about how loud the wind's gotten lately, or threatening to sic a pack of invisible creatures on me if I allow one more tree to be cut down. Perhaps she is a witch. She's certainly silly enough."

"She's not a witch. Doña Milagreta just follows the old ways," Farmer Barrido chimed in. He wasn't entirely certain how he'd ended up taking part in this meeting. He was only passing by, looking for his missing calf, when he got swept up in the tide of the Business Council. He decided to stay when they handed round the cake.

"Seemed batty enough to be a witch. Had an impressive number of warts, too. You sure she's not a witch?"

"Nope, just old," said the Farmer.

"Witch or not, she could play the part," said the Merchant. "She scared my foreman off her doorstep a few months ago. He refuses to go back. Says she gave him the evil eye. I've been trying to buy that overgrown mesquite patch she calls a farm for years. My offer was more than fair. The old hag never said a word, just squinted at him."

"Cataracts." The Farmer reached for another slice.

"Still," the Mayor mumbled around a mouthful of icing. "May as well pay her a visit."

Popular theory always blames witches. Gives them something for the brochures. On this site in 579, Verruga Ancyra died, leaving nothing but an infernal curse behind… Pure nonsense, of course.

When a witch dies—which is rare enough, and only if she can't help it—she leaves behind nothing but a fifty-foot crater and a whiff of brimstone. When they can swing it, most will pass away in their homes. Any self-respecting witch will just as soon destroy everything she owns than have someone else pawing at it.

The Mayor, the Magistrate, and the Merchant crowded into Milagreta's cottage, backs pressed against the walls. She sat rocking in the only available seat. Farmer Barrido arrived late, whistling as he hurried up the cart path through the trees, carrying what remained of the cake. He had warned the others it was best to put their jackets on backward before walking through the woods. They only laughed, leaving him behind while he switched his clothes around. He heard one of them sneer, "Rustics and their superstitions."

Laughter echoed behind them.

Farmer Barrido stood outside the cottage in the garden with the Council of Business and three scraggly goats, listening to the proceedings through an open window. "Lovely place, señora. All you could ever need within arm's reach," Mayor Liviano said, bumping his head on a hanging pot.

"Finally come to your senses and decided to do something for the winds, have you, Mayor? Don't know why you've brought half the town with you though."

"The wind was rather loud as we passed through the woods," Magistrate Fisgón admitted in an effort to appease the old woman. "Almost as if it was screaming at us. Poor Avaro lost his new hat."

"It had a quetzal tail feather in it, too. You can only get those in Tórrida, you know." The Merchant smoothed wisps of hair across his shining head, looking quite ashen. He could have sworn the wind in the woods hissed, calling him a bald, old fool as it stole his hat. And he certainly didn't like the way Milagreta was squinting at him, the lines on her face stretching as she grinned.

"Dangerous walkin' through these woods once you've given 'em reason to be angry with you."

Mayor Liviano smiled at the others; a woman this mad was surely a witch. "You have lived alone up here for a very long time, haven't you, señora?"

"Since before I was born."

"Have you ever known any, uh, shall we say... magical folk?"

"What? You mean duendes and the like? Sure, there's one that lives in the walls. Dumb as a stump and twice as useless. Can't make coffee to save his life. But, ever since that one," she nodded sharply at Merchant Avaro, "started chopping down trees there's been lots more of 'em comin' round, all riled up about the destruction of their homes."

"Lovely, lovely... I noticed you had some interesting herbs in your garden... What about witches?" The mayor would have leaned forward suggestively if he'd had room. Milagreta's chair was rocking a steady beat into his kneecap as it was.

"What? You mean the sedge? That's for the goats. If you're not here to do something for the winds, I don't know why you bothered coming at all. Now, if you'll—"

"Señora Milagreta, please, we need your help. The city needs your help. Waylay is such a lovely little place. Of course, you know, having lived here for so long."

"Get to it, Mayor."

"We want to find a way to bring people here, to see how truly lovely Waylay is."

"Bring money, you mean."

"What? No, not just money." The town fathers laughed stiffly. "It's just, other cities have such wonders… None of them are as deserving—nor their people as good—as Waylay. Wouldn't you agree?"

The town fathers shifted uncomfortably in the stretching silence as Milagreta rocked, unsure whether she was pondering her answer, finished with the conversation, or simply hadn't heard the Mayor's question. Farmer Barrido didn't trust the sharp way Milagreta's left eyebrow raised as she rubbed her chin before she finally began to speak.

"You'll want something amazing…"

"Stupendous," suggested the Mayor.

"Never been seen before."

"Yes," cried the Magistrate.

"That folks'll cross oceans to see…"

"Indeed," the Merchant concurred.

"And stick around for a while."

"A week, at least," agreed all three.

"And spend loads of money."

"Yes! Baaah!" A joyful chorus echoed from the committee gathered outside.

"All for the benefit of the most deserving, hardest working members of the Waylay citizenry."

"Why, señora Milagreta, I think you understand us better than we understand ourselves."

"True words, Mayor." She rocked in silence for several minutes more, squinting at each man in turn. "Farmer Barrido's the only one of you with enough sense to dress himself correctly. I'll talk to him. Rest of you can leave."

Over the next week, Farmer Barrido managed communications between señora Milagreta's cottage in the hills and the Mayor's office. The complicated negotiations left no time for planting, leaving his wife alone to pick up his slack.

"Alright, Farmer. I've decided," Milagreta announced one morning. "It'll be a fountain."

"A fountain?" The Farmer was underwhelmed.

"Ain't just any fountain. Huge, three tiers. Real artistic-like. And when it's done, I'll put an enchantment on it."

"What kind of enchantment? You aren't really a witch... are you?"

"Trade secret." Milagreta grinned, tapping the side of her nose.

The Farmer rushed down the hill, through the woods and to the Mayor's office. The Council of Business unanimously approved.

"I'm goin' to use only local artisans to build it," Milagreta decreed.

The Mayor agreed. "Wonderful for civic morale. Nothing better than quality Waylay-made goods."

"Any and all future repairs must be carried out by the original artisans or their apprentices."

"Absolutely. Proper upkeep will be essential," said the Merchant.

"And they must be paid a fair wage for such a high level of craftsmanship."

"I agree. A man should be compensated for his craft," the Magistrate told the Farmer.

The next morning, as the farmer entered her front gate, Milagreta called out, "Folks still tend to toss coins into fountains, don't they? For luck and such?"

The Farmer, having never been further from his farm than the hills above her cottage and having never seen a fountain, shrugged. "I'm not sure. I think so."

"Well, you tell 'em they can't touch the coins once they're in the water. Not so much as one centavo. Else the spell'll be broken. Then they'll be left with nothing but a fancy looking pond for their tourists to stare at."

Over the following days, Milagreta added a few more stipulations to the contract. She would manage the workers. She would have complete control over the design. She would write a piece about the fountain for the mayor to read during the ceremony, every word as is. Put it in the brochures, too. Finally, she would only complete the magic once the Merchant stopped all logging in the woods around her cottage. She was especially firm on that stipulation.

The Mayor and the Magistrate agreed, having grown attached to the idea of an enchanted fountain and lacking any other options. As long as it was built in the plaza in front of his inn and general store, the Merchant was likely to agree to anything. Besides, there were plenty of trees on far less steep hills. Work began the following Monday.

Like all forests in Reycaido, the Whispering Wood was home to stories. Stories like duendes and sylphs and dryads. Stories aren't like money. Even though you can trade them, you can't hold them in your hand, and it's impossible to lose them once you've given them away. Stories make a habit of lingering at the edges of your mind, leaping out when you least expect them.

Most people in Waylay claimed to no longer believe in the old stories. All the same, many villagers would turn their clothes backward, keep quiet and stick to the paths through the woods, the way their abuelas taught them to. Just because you no longer believe in something doesn't mean it can't jump out and harm you.

"'*The Fountain of the Dancing Winds*?' Sounds like nonsense to me."

"It's perfect. Just what the tourists expect." The Merchant reminded himself to have portraits made of the fountain, something bright and colorful he could slap on trinkets.

"A fountain, though? Will people really travel far from home to see a bit of water spray in the air?"

The Magistrate read from the statement Milagreta wrote for the ceremony, "'*Driven from her home as warden of the Whispering Woods, the sylph of the fountain found solace...*'"

"What's a sylph?" interrupted the Mayor.

"It's that satiny material they make women's undergarments out of in Naria," the Merchant added with certainty. "Costs at least 10 aurics a yard."

Farmer Barrido cleared his throat before telling the assembled town fathers, "Milagreta says a sylph is a nature spirit of some sort. Wind, I think. Some folks say the Whispering Wood is filled with them."

"What's it look like?"

"Invisible, I think."

"Oh ho, she's quite clever, that witch of ours," said the Merchant. "I'll have to put up more shelves in the store. Maybe I can rent space on the plaza to food vendors."

The Magistrate picked up where he left off, "*The sylph of the fountain found solace in the enchanting music of the ancient fountain. Every evening, just as the day's fading light hits the water, she can be seen dancing, grateful to the people of Waylay for providing her salvation.*"

"It doesn't look very ancient though." The Farmer looked out on the square. A ring of clean white bricks and a tangle of pipes were the sum of the fountain's progress. The mason's wife,

Adalina, stooped over, slapped mortar on a brick, then added it to the ring.

"Artistic license, my boy. The tourists expect it."

"It is odd though," the Mayor mused. "You never see anyone actually working on it, do you? The craftsmen must be terribly busy to keep sending their wives and daughters to do the job."

"Plumber's daughter was out here yesterday morning. Y'know, the one with a face like a burro. Out there laying down pipes, bless her. Must be why it looks such a horrible mess. I'm sure Plumber Brida will be along later to fix her work. Such a good father."

"It is good of him. Makes the ladies feel like they're helping."

"Admirable," said the Mayor.

"Indeed," said the Merchant.

"Hmm," said the Farmer.

The town fathers crowded on the bandstand. A banner stretched across the plaza above them. It read: *"Welcome to Waylay! Home of the Fountain of the Dancing Winds."*

All around the square, tables sagged with food and goods for sale. The baker's daughters sold colorful slices of cake and concha bread. Doña Talavera's table was piled high with hand- painted tiles, each sporting an image of the fountain. The Farmer waved at his wife from the bandstand. She stood behind a pile of hand-woven blankets. He wondered when she'd found the time to make them. Their children scooped agua fresca from a sparkling glass bowl. Only 2 cobres a cup.

A reporter had arrived on the train from Regia. The Mayor and the Merchant each took an arm and dragged him around the circumference of the square, interpreting points of interest in the tile mosaic ringing the fountain. They took turns dictating precisely what he should write.

As the sun neared the western horizon, Mayor Liviano climbed the bandstand and signaled to the band. After a quick fanfare from the trumpet, he began. "Citizens, visitors and friends, allow me to welcome you to the great unveiling of the jewel of Waylay… the Fountain of the Dancing Winds." He said a great many words on behalf of the town fathers before reading from Milagreta's statement. He had just reached the line, "she can be seen dancing—" when a gasp came from the crowd.

"Look, Mama," a tiny voice cried.

In the pool of the fountain an arm, a leg, half of a head moved about tentatively. The shape seemed to be made from the water itself. Footsteps splashed in the basin, nearing the central tower, gaining form as it moved. A shapely woman stood in the fountain's spray; her silhouette traced by the falling water. Golden rays of the lowering sun flashed silver on her graceful frame. The onlookers gasped as she twirled once, twice.

"Oh, um, ladies and gentlemen, treasured guests, may I present to you the sylph of the Whispering Woods." Everyone clapped and cheered. The sylph spun faster in the fountain. Droplets of water flew from her hair onto the crowd. A member of the band, the violinist perhaps, began playing a waltz and the other instruments joined in. The sylph danced in time to the music. Children formed couples and waltzed along in the plaza. Before the last note faded into the evening, the sylph was gone.

The town fathers milled around the bandstand, shaking hands and pinning ribbons on each other's lapels until the fabric sagged. Even the Merchant smiled as his fellows poked holes in his fine Reycaidon wool suit. The Farmer grinned, dizzy and confused as he ricocheted around accepting congratulations. All agreed their hard work had been worth it. What a marvelous success.

Milagreta sat in her cottage, rocking and thinking. A strong wind blew the door wide. Plates rattled as the door slammed against the wall.

"Oops. I'm sorry. Didn't break anything, did I?" A hazy female-shaped illusion filled the doorway, distorting the weak light from the moon.

"Stop dripping on my rug, Tromba, you old windbag, and get in here. How'd it go?"

"Good, I think. Lots of people were there. I danced a waltz." A derby hat with a bright green quetzal feather floated off the table to rest atop an invisible head as it danced around Milagreta's chair.

"Sit down. Have a cup of weak coffee. You've earned it." She knew the sylph couldn't drink it, but magical folk always appreciated the hospitality.

The hat and a battered mug hovered in front of the fire. "The moment I stepped out of the water, they started throwing coins. Especially the men. It seemed they thought coins would bring me back."

"Hmm. Maybe occasionally you should stick around, give 'em an extra twirl or two. Encore sort of thing. That is, if the fools throw enough money in."

"I think tomorrow I'll dance a polka."

"Don't forget, tomorrow's the new moon." Milagreta handed her friend a large burlap flour sack. "You can go back around midnight and gather the coins when they can't see you."

"Y'know, I had a look around before, while the silly man was talking. The workers really did a lovely job. Please give the ladies my compliments."

The old woman nodded. "It's a shame those men think a woman can only accomplish wonders if she's got magic on her side. Makes me almost wish I actually was a witch, just so I could curse them properly."

"Oh, but you should have seen it, Milagreta," the sylph said, dancing around the room again. "The brick just glows in the sunlight. The water sprays higher than I imagined it would. And the tile is beautiful. Doña Talavera even included a scene of my woods. I'm in it, with my hat."

"I've asked all of 'em—Doña Talavera, Adalina Cantero, Dorita Brida and the others—to come around next week. The ladies deserve a little something extra for their hard work. I think we should give part of the first collection of coins to them."

A sudden hot, dry gust rattled around the cottage, tipping the old woman's chair back. "Don't you worry. Everything else will still go toward buying up the land around your woods. Before you know it, our Whispering Woods will be protected from fools like that Merchant. And it'll all be thanks to his own greed."

# A MEAL IN THE MAELSTROM

## By A. Howitt

*There are monsters in the deep, great beasts that swim*
*amid sluggish ships of commerce and war,*
*and feast upon brave sailors,*
*turning the sea red with their blood.*

**Codex Maritimum**

UPON SWOLLEN CRESTS ROILING in a tempest of seaborne anger I bathe my spirit (and indeed my scaly, barnacle-covered posterior) in the last vestiges of sunlight peeking through an ash-filled sky. Time has always been on my side, but perhaps it is no longer. From the brink of hysteria next to a humming oracle stone I watch an ill-fated world shudder and groan. After months of exhaustive contemplation I've reached a troubling conclusion—this planet might well be screwed.

First to awaken my curiosity about the impending calamity was an indefinite dreamer named Flynn Silvermist. He roused me from a peaceful slumber when his voice emanated from the iridescent, pinkish stone upon the craggy island at the storm's eye. He apparently had questions regarding the fate of the world and thought to solicit answers from madness. A palpable delirium radiates from the deceptively pretty object—visions and transmissions that tickle the senses and torment the mind—and Silvermist got more than he bargained for when he queried the future-seeing stone.

The oracle stone nearly tore his fragile intellect apart when he communed with it, seeking to speak with the gods themselves. I've heard it said that the Maelstrom once belonged to the gods—their home upon the face of the world. If that's true, they've boarded their divine ferries of light and abandoned their followers, because I've never seen any evidence of their presence.

Silvermist survived coalescing with the corrupting curio, mostly because I was drawing plenty of its power and thereby sparing him the brunt of the psychic vexation. I heard his thoughts, though, his prayers to the deities. And even as a denizen of the raging vortex prognosticated to eventually devour reality, I was dismayed.

Perhaps the woodland folk knew what danger was building before anyone else—reading the fate of the world in rocky tremblings and tree-speak (or whatever nonsense the elves practice these days). For at least a century the land had been peaceful in every way a genesitically-segregated world could be considered so. Everyone kept to their own people and within the borders of their respective lands and intermingling *never* happened (except where wizards intruded upon the everyday lives of unsuspecting backwoods folk, or when prophetic nonsense spurred otherwise unimpressive individuals into acts of heroism...or *gag* *quests!*).

After I placated the elf (spouting in a godly voice some rubbish advice to him I no longer recall), it occurred to me that perhaps the stirrings of what the northern berserkers call Rag-in-a-rock may actually hold some minuscule verisimilitude. Then again, half-dressed giant-bred mutants with horns adorning their helms didn't instill me with confidence—not enough to embrace their simplistic mythology with any earnestness. And why the horns? It would be in some small way flattering if the destitute, downtrodden creatures lifted their aspirations out of the muck for a moment to venerate the supreme paragons of creation (dragons, like me, of course), but I rather suspect they presume instead to extol cattle.

And so it was that the shattering eruption of the dark mountain was portended—first by the elf scholars and more recently by the less fate-cognizant inhabitants of this world, leading to a sense of urgency and some scrambling on the part of the primitive cultures.

I simply can't be the only one among the greater beings who feels nervous about the black tendrils that stain the sky—not because I believe the volcano's imminent eruption will affect the security of my domain, but because I'm fond of my easy existence and have grown fat and comfortable in my middle age. Where should I find food when the badlands are covered in ash and the simple folks' crops in the clannish north fail, causing great populations to die off?

No humans—no horses, or cattle, or...well...*humans*, to eat. I'd be left with only what I could scrounge from the ocean, and I've never considered cold, wet seafood a delicacy. It might have served our distant ancestors fine, if indeed sea dragons ever truly enjoyed the lifestyle handed down by the ancient ones. I put forth in all reasonableness that our lives increased in quality the moment men set out upon their wooden crafts to cross this great sea and sank just as readily. They provided my ancestors with a rich food source that fueled our evolution from modest sea serpents (sometimes considered extrinsic cousins of land dragons) to supreme masters of the waterways.

I'm not angry that some dark lord has enslaved a volcano and taken it upon himself to rid the world of light and love and amiable little creatures of almost no consequence in the ambiguous scheme of things—I'm downright livid he'd dare take away my favorite food source!

So, I began watching, observing not only the dark lands where the ill-fated mountain rises from a shadowy forest of ancient curses, coughing a steady stream of pollution into the air, but also the western lands where men thrive in small villages and great cities, fattening their livestock and themselves to never-before-seen proportions.

With one eye on my food stock and the other on the growing danger, I spun a magic as old as time, drawing power from the endlessly roiling waters around me. Since the day I crawled from a soft-skinned, gooey egg and scrambled on tiny fin-covered legs toward the sea, with hundreds of identical blue-green siblings, I've been wrapped up in a race for survival, eating all I could and growing as fast as my form could manage. Shed scales layer my craggy demesne and the ocean floor below, a testament to how long I've been in the unending storm—if I had to guess, three centuries or more—all the while, biding my time until my inevitable thaumaturgical awakening.

For most sea dragons, it's the instinct to mate that brings about the change, the desire to lie on a sandy beach and roar sorcery until the air flickers with electricity—light shows that prove one's virility to prospective mates. For me, it was the anger engaged when I learned my preferred food may soon die out. I called to the great winds that pull flotsam ever into the storm's eye, where it collects in the oracle stone's manic halo. I called to the sea, and I wove together a magic so ancient it has no name. Veins of energy prickled through my hide, setting muscles twitching and my teeth tingling, until I was compelled to swim the migratory pattern ingrained in my memory. And that was when I made my move.

Unlike my land-born cousins, I have no wings, only dorsal fins (beautiful enough to make any butterfly or pegasus envious), so a swim it had to be. With theurgy coursing through my body, I left familiar territory, my refuge of safety, and headed out to ruin someone's day.

My first destination was one of the craggy isles on the northern archipelago, home of the ancient ones. It wasn't that I thought my kin would have specific answers for me, but I hoped they might share my concerns. As a contemplative example of my kind, I aimed to reason with my rather simple relatives and gain their support in my attempt to salvage our future. But, you know, family reunions are often just one of those things...

When I approached the choppy waters that drag vessels into the rocks, vanquishing stouthearted sea captains, the lightning displays were already in full force. While the weather patterns of the microclimate often accounted for unusual phenomena in the bay, I knew immediately that magic was responsible for the light show that day. The evidence of a mating ritual in full swing greeted me, an unwelcome assault to my senses that I'm not ashamed to admit I didn't miss during my extended reclusive respite. Roars from more than two-dozen orgy participants filled the air, calls of invitation and warning all rolling together into a discordant cacophony.

One great big serpent lay on their side, upon a relatively flat little rocky island. As they were the apparent eldest among those gathered, I made a beeline for their location. No stranger to sea dragon customs I crept close, bowing my head, creating an appropriately graceful curve in my long neck. I even swept my tail from side to side, flashing cerulean fins so they caught the gleam of the lightning arcing above. It seemed to do the trick.

The elder one raised their wide head and opened their jaw, emitting three sharp, screechy barks to tell me my advance was agreeable. I didn't want to give the wrong impression (either that I was there to challenge for supremacy or to fornicate), so I stopped some distance away and plopped my hindquarters on the shelf, waiting and considering how best to phrase my query. Looking back, I probably should have begun with some version of an apology for breaching custom, but it didn't occur to me until after I'd opened my mouth.

"A thousand pardons," I said, using the mellifluous but oft-considered anachronous acrolect of the ancient ones. "Great elder, I beg an audience. It has come to my attention that perhaps a contingency plan is in order."

The elder abandoned all welcoming gestures and clawed deep tracks in the slab below. Their reply came in the guttural, coarse sea serpent tongue, "Contingency plan?"

"Yes," I continued, adopting the common vernacular, loathing every velar consonant. "A secondary plan…for when the first fails?"

"I know what a contingency plan is," the elder snapped. Little zings of purple and blue electricity veined from their snout up two impressive horns ridged by countless age rings. "What sort of plan does one need in order to copulate?" They started forward.

I considered for a long moment how to answer without insult, but as the great blue body drew near, dwarfing me and arcing galvanism between our scales, I felt a sudden need to speak— to deflect attention from me and onto my concern. What came from my mouth was probably in hindsight the wrong thing. "I'm not here to copulate, but to talk about food."

"Then you've come to the wrong reef," the saucy elder said, sidling up to me and draping a heavy tail around my hindquarters. "Some of us have been here for weeks. Does it look like we're concerned with a meal?"

I might have overreacted.

In fact, I'm sure I did.

"But that's just it," I said, in a frantic attempt to assert my crucial consideration while dodging the senescent dragon's affection, "we may find ourselves on the wrong side of a losing battle with hunger, and I for one—"

The elder's tail knocked into me, rattling against my ribs and crumpling my second dorsal fin. I couldn't breathe. The violence didn't stop there. Claws lashed out and if not for my superior nimbleness, I might have been scored from foreleg to haunch. Okay, maybe I exaggerate, but I scooted right out of the way and decided my visit to my hatching-place was over.

As I skedaddled back to the water, the aged tyrant had a few unkind things to say, mostly warnings never to return and the like, but also a comment about the prurient nature of the reef gathering that—had I not already been repulsed by the thought of mating—would have sealed the deal.

Back through the tide, avoiding the frothy evidence of my kin's carnal soiree, I went. It was time to come up with a better plan. Obviously, the sea dragons couldn't be bothered to take up concern for feeding the next generation—only creating it.

The northmen's home was the closest destination for a satisfying meal, but having already been agitated by one hoary despot, I sought an alternative. I wasn't interested in a fight—and if there's one thing the horn-helmed folks there like, it's a fight. With my stomach rumbling its discontent, I rode the current of the outer Maelstrom down south, where the cool northern waters intermingle with warmer waters in merchant shipping lanes.

A relative dearth of large prey during the night never prohibited me forlornly trolling the empty waves, hoping to get lucky. But that evening I was pleasantly surprised to find a lone ship just outside the definitively strong current. Clever captain, whomever he was—staying just beyond the Maelstrom's grasp. I surfaced to get a better view.

Lucky indeed, it was a military vessel! On the surface, that might sound like a contradiction—my desire to see armed men in what would ordinarily be a merchant domain—but where merchants keep crew numbers low to greedily fill their holds with goods like tea and silk rugs (both of which taste terrible), military ships contain soldiers. Lots of them. And I'll let you in on a little secret: once you peel the metal covering off, they're just as easy on the gut as merchants.

Relying on my ears and tongue to guide me (because eyesight might be considered a sea dragon's only weakness), I drew astern the craft and got a good hold on her rear end. I might not have all the weight behind me of my fire-breathing cousins, but I yanked hard enough to rock the vessel and tear away the hinged rudder.

A bell clanged—a dinner bell in my mind. Shouts erupted from the deck and lanterns scurried about, heading for the afflicted part of the ship. While they investigated the damaged stern, I ducked under the surface and swam for the newly unmanned bow.

Mine wasn't the sort of elegant attack painted on navigation maps (sea dragons aren't really long enough to coil around a ship, though we've never complained about the fear-conjuring depictions), but what I lacked in brawn, I made up for in artistry. Hauling myself up a garish land-dragon figurehead (an irony not lost on me), I scrabbled to the deck and tore at the first mast that supported the agility sails. With those and the rudder out of commission, the ship would be adrift, primed for a harvest that could take hours.

As I headed back to the water, I aimed a particularly impressive blast of voltage at a trio of sailors foolish enough to shine their lights over the gunwale to ascertain what manner of monster molested their vessel.

They fell into the sea and I opted to fill my stomach while the remaining ill-fated crewmen scrambled on deck. It was only as the sky lightened, telling me a ruddy, ash-streaked dawn was near, that I debated whether to continue my feast or retreat home. Without cover of darkness, I was at a disadvantage—an easy target if they were armed with harpoons. However, I was still invested in storing up my fat layer, and with the dark mountain's fury escalating, the shipping lanes might fall into disuse.

Out of the water, I clambered up the timbers, awaiting an opportunity to grab sailors over the gunwale. Unfortunately, dawn's first rays revealed another craft making its way toward our position and as it neared, its golden lion banner informed me that it must be one of the king's ships—which provoked my further inspection of the damaged vessel. It boasted tall, gnarled masts I hadn't noticed in the night, and a pale wolf on a black banner—it hailed from the Darkwoods, the shadowed lands below the jagged peaks that smoked damning signals to the world.

Well, shit. It was time for me to leave.

I dug my claws into the wood and snaked my way around the side of the ship, staying out of sight and avoiding the cannons. Slipping into the sea, I distanced myself from both vessels as they predictably opened fire, chain shot clanking and tearing into sails.

Flexing superior naval might, the lion ship turned and loosed what sounded like a full barrage of cannonballs. All but the smallest sea critters scattered, leaving a school of tiny silver-striped fish enjoying an early plankton breakfast, and me. My stomach, only half-full, sent a very convincing appeal to override my circumspection, but conclusively, my curiosity won out over good sense. I surfaced, riding the tide with my nostrils, eyes, and ears above water.

The air was tense and filled with the odor of gunpowder and smoke. If I just waited, one of the ships would join me in the briny blue. My bet was on the lion banner ship, despite their opening display of hostility. Everyone knew darkwood was tough—maybe tough enough to keep the wolf banner craft afloat until it destroyed the smaller vessel (it certainly withstood my attempts to drag it down).

The invaders' answer to the king's greeting came fast and loud—a retort of violent disapproval and aggression. They fired back. Cannons burped flame from their muzzles and a foggy haze rolled upward in a disguising curtain.

It looked as though I'd be the winner for sure! I could barely contain my excitement. But then, the lion vessel did something unexpected—something I'd never seen before. More than a dozen puffs of smoke erupted from the deck and trails of flame lit the sky, zooming toward the darkwood ship.

Explosions sounded as the missiles struck their target, plunging into beams and boards. A hailstorm of fire. If I hadn't been so unnerved by the searing red balls of heat flying around, I might have enjoyed the show before the feast just a little more.

Sailors leapt overboard, splashing. Each slap of skin on water pricked my delicate ears, whetting my appetite. I was tempted to head straight in to scoop up my prizes, but knowing the missiles were being reloaded, I hesitated.

Damn my curious nature. I skirted the side of the king's ship, heading for the bow—not too hastily. I didn't want to get caught in the crossfire.

"A devastating hit!" a voice cried above me. "Well done."

"Shall I give the order again, sir?" another man asked.

"No, not just yet."

"Let her burn and we'll send out the ropes," the enthusiastic third voice said. "She's dead in the water, sir."

Dead in the water—music to my ears. More splashes sounded. I'd have to be quick to harvest my prey before the lion vessel got too close.

"Eastern marauders," the first voice said, presumably the leader giving orders. "After this scouting party, you can bet there'll be more on the way." A slam sounded. "Send a message back to the castle. Tell them we've spotted a darkwood ship, a suspected outrider that may indicate an invasion."

An invasion of the king's waterways? How delightfully

unexpected. I was torn. While men drowned just outside of sight but still within earshot, I was glued to the underside of the lion vessel, eavesdropping on an intriguing exchange.

"Aye, sir," the less important fellow said.

"Send word to Robert Nutwell, Lord High Admiral of His Majesty's Sea. We're riding this buxom lass east, in haste. Beseech His Lordship to send more frigates to follow. Fast ones, with plenty of shot." He chuckled. "Long, the Maelstrom has protected our seaward border, but with the mountains smoking, war is on the horizon. I can feel it in my bones."

"I can feel it too, sir! But are you sure skirting this close to the Maelstrom is a good idea? Ships disappear in there."

Sir, whomever he was, grumbled something under his breath that even my sensitive ears couldn't decipher, but then he spoke louder. "Clever villains. They tried to sneak in through this infernal death trap, to take us by surprise. They're planning something, mark my words. Before long, dozens will come."

One could hope. I stole away from the ship's side—the sounds that men make directly preceding death being somewhat too hard to ignore any longer.

"You'll see," Sir said. "My father warned me about a shift in the east—powerful sorcerers and lords of magic, risen from the ashes of a dying volcano, or perhaps called there by its fury. He told me of a great evil born from the fire."

If Sir kept talking, I didn't hear the rest of it. I dipped and sped for the drowning men.

As I snaked through the waves, tearing pieces off the dead and dying, sating my ravenousness, I might have inserted a sort of elegant flamboyance to my underwater dance. Blood clouded the water and as soon as I'd eaten my fill, I quit the shipping lane and swam further into the drag, where no ships could follow. The sonorous hum of the oracle stone welcomed me home as I skirted the sharp reef and crawled back up the rocky slab. I slumped onto my side to aid the heroic effort my stomach was making. War between the king lion and the eastern wolves—I couldn't have asked for a more propitious eventuality.

Though black bands of death rent the sky, and volcanic and magical mayhem threatened existence, the humans were apparently committed to feeding me. They'd send ships. Lion and wolf would jockey for position, pushing ever closer to the Maelstrom's tenacious grasp, and the men who once so providently avoided my range would voluntarily enter.

And I would await them. Welcome them with open arms and an open mouth.

The only trickiness of the situation seemed in keeping the war a secret from my befuddled, sex-crazed kin. If they caught on, I might be evicted and the mad stone's crag might become the next breeding beach, befouled and smutted, not to mention scorched.

No, that wouldn't do.

I had work to accomplish, plans to formulate, and most of all, a pressing need for an extensive repose.

# MOTHER EARTH HAS A PLAN

## By Kelly Matsuura

A HORDE OF FIFTY-PLUS zombies staggered forward; some were freshly dead, others practically skeletons, but they were all hungry.

As were we—our group of seven had last eaten four days ago. But unlike the zombies, there was no food in sight for us.

"We're surrounded!" Joel waved his blunt knife around desperately.

We formed a circle, weapons facing out.

Except for me. I didn't even draw my dagger from its sheath.

"This is it," I muttered, surprisingly calm. I was just done. For me, the undead had won. I had no fight left. I was mentally prepared to join the roaming corpses.

The horde advanced.

"Don't give up!" Chris urged everyone. "We'll fight our way through!"

However, as the zombies closed in, the earth trembled below our feet.

"What the—" Steve began, but was immediately sucked down below ground before he could finish his curse.

Joel and several others followed—disappearing in seconds.

I too felt the ground open below my feet and suck me down.

At first, it felt suffocating, like the soil filled every space around me. Then, my feet touched solid ground again and a breeze blew the dirt from my cheeks.

"Whoa." I looked around, trying to get my bearings. "Where are we?"

My friends and I all stood agape in what appeared to be an underground cavern.

"Look, water!" Amber pointed out a steady trickle of clear water, running down the rock face. It made a lovely tinkling sound as it did so.

"Yeah!"

We rushed to wash our hands and faces, and all had a good long drink.

But as I stared at the bottom of my empty cup, I was still so desperately hungry.

Water and shelter were essential, but without food, we would have to go back out to scavenge right away. Dark thoughts crept in about giving up. I didn't have to go back out. None of us did. We could all stay here and wait for the end. On our own terms. It would be so peaceful, I thought, to just lie here in the cool, womb-like cavern. The only sound, the trickling water. Just then, Michelle called out from behind an enormous boulder.

"Guys, you've gotta come see this!"

Curious, we leaped to our feet, then passed single-file through the narrow gap between the rocks. At first, I couldn't process what I was seeing. I blinked several times. Was I dreaming this whole experience?

Sunlight streamed down from a wide opening in the rocks above, revealing a large pile of rotting zombie corpses in various stages of decomposition. But what was most surprising was they didn't smell at all, in fact, there was a pleasant aroma of soil and peat in the air.

On closer inspection, the decaying corpses were fermenting, creating layer upon layer of organic matter.

"They're being composted," Michelle explained. "I don't know how it's possible but look at the soil being produced." She held out a fistful to our noses, and we agreed with her assessment. By some miracle, the elements in the cave were producing the right balance of chemicals to actually create healthy soil, suitable for growing food.

As if this discovery wasn't weird enough, lush, leafy, plants sprouted in the dense soil, right before our eyes.

"Wow, look! They have little buds."

The yellow buds opened into small flowers, then quickly grew into a small fruit—similar to a tomato, but more purple in color. There were suddenly dozens of them ripening on the plants, just begging us to pick them.

Joel grabbed one and took a big bite. "Mmm, juicy!" he mumbled, quickly taking another bite, then another.

My stomach was rumbling along with everyone else's—I had

to try one. I hadn't eaten fresh fruit in months. This was the sweetest, most delicious thing I'd ever put into my mouth.

"It tastes like pears!" I said with the biggest grin.

We gobbled down two fruits each, then we spent a few minutes laughing and hugging, not believing our luck.

They all looked to me as the group leader.

With real hope, at last, I found my confidence again.

"We can stay as long as we need to. Rest and recharge," I told them. "When we're stronger, we'll go look for any survivors from the old group and bring them here. Home."

As we lay down on our bedrolls and blankets, a voice echoed through the cavern.

"You are safe here. Mother Earth protects you. Stay alive, humans. The world will be yours again soon."

# APPALACHIAN
# LOVE SONGS
## By J. H. Schiller

THE MOST HUNTED CREATURE on Pine Mountain is the young Appalachian woman, and the hunter's name is Death. It comes for her in the woods as a mountain lion stalking her steps. It comes for her in the childbed when her life gushes out in a torrent of blood. It comes for her as a fever, a festering wound. And sometimes, more often than you might think, it comes for her as a man. Just read the lyrics of a few Appalachian love songs—murder ballads, they call them. You'll see.

When Death came for Lyda Miller one hot July day, it took the form of a baby's bottom wedged into the bowl of her pelvis and held there by labor pains that nigh on ripped her in two. If she'd been a little older, her narrow hips set a little wider, Shiney might have been able to turn the baby. Lord knows she'd tried every trick she had. But Lyda was only fourteen, a thin willow branch of a girl; at least, she had been before she got ruined.

Shiney rested an arthritic hand on the rigid swell of Lyda's belly.

Her gift found no spark of life from the baby—a son, he would've been, if he'd lived. And his mama was fading fast. Five decades of tending to birthing women told Shiney there was no saving her, not with how much blood she'd lost. All that remained was to ease her passing.

The old midwife rinsed her hands in a bowl of water and turned to her great-niece. "Play somethin' to take away her pain."

Rosabel wiped tears from her cheeks and tore her eyes away from Lyda's bone-white face. Not too many years ago, the two of them spent Sunday mornings under the rough-hewn pews at church, playing with their corn dollies while Reverend Blankenship raged and thundered about the fires of hell.

Girls grow up hard and fast in these parts.

Rosabel picked up her fiddle and cradled it against her chin. This particular instrument was more than just spruce and poplar. With the right song, its music could call a man's spirit to heel like a hunter with a coon dog.

A man's spirit . . . or that of a dying girl.

She drew the bow across the strings and began to play "Soldier's Joy." A lively Scottish reel might not seem a natural choice for a death watch, but Rosabel knew what she was about.

"Fifteen cents for moonshine," she sang. "Fifteen cents for beer, fifteen cents for morphine—Lord, take me away from here..."

The harsh edges of Lyda's agonized grimace softened as the music carried away her pain. Rosabel slowed the tune to match the cadence of the girl's breathing. She closed her eyes, shutting out the sight of bruised thighs and blood-soaked sheets. As the gaps between inbreaths lengthened, the music took on the melancholy weight of a dirge.

Shiney pressed her cheek to Lyda's pale forehead and found it as cool as a spring house. "It's time, Rosabel."

The melody shifted from "Soldier's Joy" to "In the Sweet By and By." Rosabel hadn't even reached the refrain when her friend passed. She watched as Lyda's shade rose, bent over the lifeless body, and straightened, cradling a baby. Rosabel played on until they faded from sight. When the last note faded into thick, deathbed silence, she lowered her fiddle and bow with shaking hands.

"Does it ever get easier?"

"No, child," Shiney said. "But we get harder." She walked to the mantel and stopped the clock, marking the time of Lyda's death. "Lord, it's already gone four thirty. You best head on over to the Bradley place." She looked down at the dead girl. "I'll clean her up and set by with her. Those brothers of hers ain't worth a tinker's damn. They'll have her in the dirt by sunrise if I don't."

Those brothers of hers were most likely what landed Lyda in the childbed. Their father had died in the coal mine, and consumption took their mother not long after. A girl on her own with those liquor-loving boys?

Well, there are some things you just don't talk about.

"I don't think I can do it, Shiney," Rosabel said. "I can't play for no weddin' dance after… I just can't."

"No choice. You told Billy Bradley you'd do it, and he ain't the kind of man who hears no."

As far as Rosabel knew, there wasn't any kind of man who'd

hear no.

*Maybe tomorrow*, or *not yet*, or *I'll think on it*. A girl could get away with saying something like that. But *no* was the most dangerous word that could pass a woman's lips.

Rosabel couldn't afford to turn Billy down anyway. He was paying her in whiskey, which Shiney needed to make herbal tonics. She sighed and slid her fiddle and bow into a felt drawstring bag. "I can come back here to set with you once't I'm done."

"No, you go on home after the dancin' winds down. Get some sleep."

Shiney took a deep breath and turned to her grim duties. She'd spoken the truth; it never got easier. Her gnarled hands had prepared many young bodies for the grave's embrace. It hurt every time.

When Rosabel opened the door to leave, Death swooped inside. A winter wren flew a fluttering circle around the room, then alit on the stopped clock and began to sing. Shiney's wide, staring eyes met hers. The old woman pressed her lips together and shook her head.

She didn't speak.

She didn't have to.

They both knew what a bird in the house foretold. Today's dying wasn't done.

Sweat streamed down Rosabel's back as her bow danced through

"Cumberland Gap," "Whiskey Before Breakfast," and "Turkey in the Straw." Nonsense songs, meant for nothing more than kicking up heels. Breathless couples spun and whirled in the stifling barn, a smile on every face. They couldn't help it—not when Rosabel played.

The boom of a shotgun startled her, bringing the song to a discordant halt. A knot of grinning, red-faced men charged into the sea of dancers carrying a fence rail. The barn filled with raucous laughter and excited yells. *Shivaree! Shivaree!*

Two fellows seized Abner Mullins and pulled him from his bride's arms. He straddled the rail, and his boisterous abductors lifted it over their heads. They trotted a stumbling circle through the crowd so everyone could yell bawdy advice to the groom. Abner's winces of pain suggested they might ought to take it easy with the jostling or his evening would be spent with a cold compress instead of a warm wife.

Speaking of wives, Katie Bradley—Katie Mullins, now— shrieked as mamas and grannies grabbed her with strong, chapped hands and plunked her down in a washtub. Katie's oldest sister, eighteen years old and hipping her third son, poured a pitcher of cold water over her head. The menfolk hefted the washtub and paraded Katie along the same route as her husband. A passel of kids followed, banging pots and pans with wooden spoons, as the bride and groom were carried out of the barn toward their newly built cabin and the marital bed. There, rowdy well-wishers would surround the home, and the merrymaking would continue as the newlyweds inside sealed their covenant in the oldest of ways.

Rosabel shook her head as she watched the procession depart. She wanted nothing to do with marriage. To her, love looked an awful lot like bonded labor. Unlike other girls her age, Rosabel had not grown up waiting on a man hand and foot. Her father ran off when she was six years old. Her mother, like Lyda, died birthing not two months later, taking a long-awaited son with her. So Rosabel was sent to live with her granny's sister Shiney, a spinster midwife, and she'd grown up free. Hell would freeze over before she'd willingly sign her soul away in a marriage contract.

But Pine Mountain girls didn't decide such things for themselves, and a certain young man had a different plan in mind for Rosabel.

Willie Collier watched as she shouldered her fiddle bag and picked up a corked jug of Billy Bradley's best corn whiskey. His eyes lingered on her black hair, which rippled down her back in glossy waves, stark against the pale yellow of her dress. Loose hair was meant to signal girlhood to would-be suitors, as women of courting age wore theirs pinned up. But with the shivaree filling Willie's mind with thoughts of the wedding night, it had the opposite effect. When he looked at Rosabel, his mind filled with visions of creamy bare skin and the haunting strains of a love song.

Willie licked his dry lips and followed her out of the barn.

"Ho there, Rosie," he called, jogging to catch up to her. "I'll walk you home."

"That's mighty kind of you," she said, "but I don't want to put you out."

What she didn't want was Willie trailing after her, Willie seeing that no lamps burned in the cabin she shared with Shiney, Willie knowing she'd be sleeping there alone.

"Ain't no bother." He fell into step beside her. "Anyways, there's somethin' I want to ask you."

Dread pooled in the pit of her stomach. "Maybe we could talk tomorrow. I been helpin' Shiney all day, and I'm wore out."

Willie felt a wave of tenderness for the girl. Rosabel had no man to look after her, to protect her, to make sure she married well. All she had was a dried-up old maid who kept her running the hills at all hours, bleaching bloody sheets and sitting up with the dead. Willie on the other hand—well, his father owned the coal mine, which made Pa the richest man on the mountain. Willie could give Rosabel pretty dresses and nice things. He could give her a roomy cabin to fill with babies. He could give her his love. What more could any woman want?

"It's happy talk," he said. "Somethin' that'll put a smile on your face."

Rosabel's bare feet fell silently on the well-worn path to the creek. Around her, lightning bugs hung in the humid air, flashing messages of love to attract mates. A chorus of crickets chirped to the same purpose. This talk with Willie would be just another mating display.

*Look at my strong back, girl,* he'd say. *Hear the jingle in my pockets. Feel the soft sheets of my bed.*

"I'd rather wait, if it's all the same to you." Rosabel watched him from the corner of her eye. She saw his lips tighten, his jaw clench. He was a man used to getting his way. She'd have to tread carefully.

"It's just… Willie, I watched Lyda Miller die today. Me and her was friends, and I'm…" She forced herself to look up at him. Moonlight gilded the tears streaking her cheeks. "I'm grievin.'"

His face relaxed, softening into a mask of pity. He took her arm, his fingers gentle but firm, and tugged her to a halt. The crickets' song ceased. All Rosabel heard over the thunder of her heart was the stream's burbling rush.

Willie cupped her chin in his hands and pressed his lips to her forehead. "I'm sorry, Rosie," he whispered.

His sense of purpose strengthened as he gazed at her stricken face. Rosabel deserved a better life, a life of ease and laughter rather than blood and tears. The poor girl was just overcome by emotion, as the fairer sex so often was. She didn't understand what he was about to offer her.

"Tell you what," Willie said, as he released her and stepped back. "I'll walk you as far as the cave spring."

Rosabel bit her lip and nodded. Grinning, Willie started up the path, leaving her to walk three steps behind in a woman's proper place. He didn't speak as they climbed the mountain, but he hummed a lilting song.

A dangerous song.

A love song.

Rosabel knew it well. Her father, whose fiddle bumped against her back as she walked, used to play it for her mother. Rosabel played it too, but only when she was by herself. Hearing it now, alone in the night with Willie Collier, stiffened the hairs at the nape of her neck.

All too soon, they crested a rise where the stream spilled from a tree-lined pool. The full moon silvered its surface, a glimmering contrast to the pitch-black cave from which the spring flowed. The path continued around the watering hole into the shadowed forest, where Shiney's cabin lay just around the bend.

Rosabel yearned to run toward refuge, but as any country girl can tell you, running just gets you chased. Instead, she steeled her nerves and said, "Thanks for the company. I'd best be gettin' on home."

"Not 'til we talk about this mornin'." He rested his hands on her shoulders, gazing at her with the hungry desire of a fox watching a fat hen.

Rosabel fought the urge to pull away. His green eyes brimmed with obsession—or was it possession?—as he again hummed the familiar refrain.

"Black is the color of my true love's hair." Willie's voice was hoarse as he whispered the lyrics. He stroked her curls, twined an ebony ringlet around his finger. "At first, I figured you didn't know I was watchin' you, but the way you moved, the way you showed yourself to me… I knew you wanted me to see."

Her breath caught, but it wasn't the thought of what he'd seen that tightened her throat. It was the sure knowledge of what he'd heard.

"You finished your bath and sat down on that rock." He pointed to a massive stone by the edge of the pool. "You was soakin' wet, nothin' on but your shift." In his mind's eye, white muslin clung to her body, tracing her curves like a lover's kiss. "Then you picked up your fiddle and played 'Black Is the Color.' That's when I knew." Willie's hands drifted down to her waist. "If old Shiney hadn't turned up to fetch you, I'd've spoke up right then."

Rosabel eased away from his eager hands. "I didn't know you was there, Willie," she said. "My hand to God, I wasn't playin' that song for you." She rested a hand on her chest. "I was playin' it for *me*."

Willie wasn't mad. Not yet.

He was stuck trying to make sense of what she was saying. A woman's power lay between her legs. Power to snare a lover. Power to bring a husband to heel. Power to give life to a squalling son. But that kind of power only mattered in relation to men. Oh, he'd heard folks whisper about Rosabel's fiddle, about the power of her music. Superstitious nonsense, if you asked him. But even if it *was* true, the idea of her using that power with no man in mind... well, it was just plain silly. Singing a love song for herself made about as much sense as tits on a bull.

She was showing him her virtue, that was all. Playing hard to get, like good girls do.

"Marry me, Rosie," he said. "You wanted me. Now, you got me."

"But this ain't what I want." The words flew out of Rosabel's mouth three heartbeats ahead of her better judgment. Willie's face darkened like a thundercloud. "Not yet, I mean." Her thoughts raced like startled rabbits as she searched for something to say. Something *safe*. "I'll talk to Shiney. I'll... I'll think on it."

He closed the distance between them in one long stride, gripped her arms so tightly she knew there'd be bruises. "Nothin' to think on."

"Listen, you ain't yourself right now, Willie. Just go on home and get some sleep. The way you feel," she said, "it'll be gone come sunup. Things'll go back to normal."

"I don't want normal," he said. "I want *you*." He reached for her and pulled her against his body, leaving no doubt in her mind about what he wanted. "Marry me."

It was not a question.

Rosabel looked up at Willie, met his fevered eyes.

And she said, "No."

The word hung between them, making enough space for her to wriggle out of his grasp. She knew it was foolish, knew it was dangerous, but saying it felt so good she said it again—louder this time.

"No!"

Quick as the strike of a rattlesnake, his big hand closed around her throat.

But Rosabel was quick, too. Before Wille's fingers could dig in and squeeze, she smacked Billy Bradley's jug of whiskey into his temple. He crumpled to the ground, and she darted away.

Most Pine Mountain girls would run home after something like that—home, where a brother, or a daddy, or a papaw would be waiting. For those girls, the best defense against a man who aimed to own you was a man who already did.

Rosabel was not most girls.

For one thing, her cabin lay empty. If she ran there, the only thing standing between her and Willie would be a door with no lock.

For another, no man owned her, and none ever would.

Willie pushed up to all fours, shaking his head like a stag in rut. Rosabel waded into the pool, resisting the lure of panicked flight. She held her fiddle over her head as she slogged through the chest-deep water. One wrong step, and she'd lose her music.

One wrong step, and she'd lose her life.

She'd no sooner clambered out into the cave on the far side than Willie roared and charged in after her. He slipped and fell, clumsy on the slimy stones, but he popped right back up again. She had a minute, two at most, before he reached her—and if he reached her, he'd have his way.

Rosabel slid her fiddle free and began playing "Omie Wise." It was a slow song, a murder ballad in memory of a slain woman from Randolph County. But she played it fast and desperate. The words flowed through her mind as her bow danced.

*Hear me, oh hear me, I'll tell you no lies*

*As I sing of John Lewis killin' sweet Omie Wise.*

"You're mine, Rosie!" Willie bellowed.

He'd already reached the center of the pool. He had her now; he could feel it. Of course, he couldn't marry her, not anymore. A man can't marry a woman with *no* on her lips. A woman like that's no good. A woman like that won't be missed.

The clatter of pebbles drew Willie's eyes away from Rosabel. A girl had appeared in the mouth of the cave. Her stomach bulged under a torn blue dress, and water dripped from her cornsilk hair.

Willie froze, dumbfounded.

Rosabel's music echoed from the black cave, carrying the tale of Omie Wise. How her lover abandoned her with a baby in her belly. How he lured her to Adams' Spring with promises of love. How he drowned her and left her to rot.

Then the tune changed to "Tom Dooley," the story of another murdered woman—this one stabbed to death on a North Carolina mountaintop. Tom's doomed sweetheart, Laura Foster, stepped to the water's edge. She wore a gore-streaked white dress, and a wicked blade gleamed in her right hand.

Willie wanted to back away, wanted to flee, but the music held him fast. He listened, helpless, as the song changed again.

"Down in the Willow Garden" called forth Rose Connelly and a cup of poisoned wine.

A few bars of "Poor Ellen Smith" summoned a slip of a lass with a hunting rifle on her shoulder.

Then Rosabel walked ankle-deep into the pool, her fiddle cradled under her chin, playing "Knoxville Girl." A young woman with a crushed skull joined the others.

She kept playing as the dead women waded into the water.

She kept playing as Willie turned and ran, skidded and splashed.

She kept playing as Omie Wise dragged him down, as Laura Foster stabbed him, as each woman took her vengeance—a victim no more. Rosabel didn't lower her bow until the pool was still and the shades had returned to wherever they slept and dreamt of bloody justice.

The trilling call of a screech owl shattered the silence, calling to mind the winter wren from Lyda's cabin.

Death's work here was done.

Again, Rosabel held her fiddle high as she crossed the pool. No grasping fingers plucked at her. No shouting voice accused her. She thought she saw Willie's face beneath the surface, but it was only the white circle of the full moon's reflection.

His body would surface soon enough. Drowned and stabbed. Shot and poisoned. Beaten and bludgeoned.

Though the spring was within spitting distance of her cabin, Rosabel wasn't worried about what people might think. She was just a woman, after all—a girl, really—with no man to look after her.

Yes, the women of Pine Mountain know what it is to be hunted.

But hunted isn't the same as helpless.

# POSEIDON COMES TO HEAL

## By Sidney Stevens

BARRY DEVRIES STOOD ON the viewing platform overlooking Waukunah Springs. It was his favorite time of day—after the busloads of tourists left, just him and dozens of West Indian manatees floating still and silent like portly submarines in the aquamarine waters of their warm winter sanctuary.

This evening, though, the scene brought no peace. Barry stuffed down irritation. This was his winter sanctuary too—here at Henry T. Moss Lagoon State Park—his home from January through April for the past three years, where he volunteered as a guest greeter and park maintenance man. His job was to answer endless questions about manatees, preserve the park's natural "old Florida" ambiance, and hopefully teach his wife a lesson.

Clearly, that last task wasn't working. Deb's indecision about retiring seemed no closer to resolution. Barry sighed loudly. Just the latest maneuver in her accelerating turn against him.

From across the springs, a large manatee began moving in

his direction—the one he called Finn, nearly thirteen feet long and probably upwards of three thousand pounds. The creature slipped through the water, flippers and tail steadily propelling his corpulent body as if Barry's furious thoughts had sounded a silent summons. He surfaced once, snorted gently, and resubmerged. A masterclass in equanimity.

If only Barry's life could remain so unruffled. Brats—that's what Deb called her middle-school students. Brats, for God's sake. Yet she lived for them. Hell, Deb lived for them more than she lived for him.

Barry's jaw clenched. Of course, he'd return to Michigan to resume his marriage at the end of April, as he always did. He wasn't a quitter or turncoat. Not like so many others who'd thwarted and belittled him over the years. He had a list—one that increasingly included Deb. His wife was the one person he'd always counted on, the center of his everything. Where had that Deb gone?

Barry's throat filled with something bitter and hard. He quickly gulped it down and watched Finn floating burdenless in the clear water below. God, what he'd give for that life. Not possible, of course. There was no question he'd go back to Deb—be the bigger person, the better person. Take the high road. But he'd also continue devoting his winters to warmth and manatees. What else did Deb expect him to do? She'd be sorry one day if she let him go.

Barry squeezed out of the shower the next morning to a text

from Deb. Why the hell did he buy this cramped old Airstream, anyway? Used piece of junk. He donned his gold-rim glasses—the same rectangular style he'd worn since high school—and skimmed the text: "Parent meeting and book group tonight. Talk at nine?"

Barry ran a hand over his balding head. Just how was he supposed to respond? "No problem—I'll wait dutifully and patiently till you're free." Was that what she wanted to hear?

Barry yanked on khaki cargo shorts that hung to his knees (damn stumpy legs), black ankle socks, worn leather hiking boots (size 5), and a large olive-green polo shirt bearing the Waukunah Springs logo of a grinning manatee. He tucked the extra length into his shorts, tightened his belt under his round belly, and slapped on his Waukunah Springs cap (emblazoned with the same grinning manatee). Then he texted a curt "Sure" and trudged from the campground to the park office to help Carl, the park ranger, open for the day.

Deb would definitely be sorry she played so fast and loose with their nightly calls. Not that Barry couldn't do more to nurture their connection—grant greater flexibility in their call schedule or occasionally fly home for face-to-face communion. But then Deb would win. He couldn't—wouldn't—allow that, not after she'd thwarted his dream to move to Florida. Once, it had been their dream together. Then it stalled. She stalled.

Barry's boots crunched on the mulch path, each step escalating the tension in his head. "Not ready to retire." That's what Deb said just last week. "Still have something to give...Can't imagine anything more meaningful." She'd planted her flag—yet again—

and now he was supposed to just watch it wave in the wind? Like a damn sheep?

This is what 'blowing your top off' felt like. Getting steamed up. Feeling your blood boil. Seeing red. Barry felt them all deep inside—and so much more. He could barely suck in enough air sometimes to keep his lungs inflated. Like he was suffocating, drowning in his own life.

Barry paused to collect himself before pushing open the office door.

Carl glanced up. "Good, you're here ... Manatee coming today from Jacksonville Zoo for release."

Barry felt himself lighten. His favorite task: Helping recovering manatees acclimate back to the wild.

"Unusual case," Carl said. "Got tangled in a fishing line ... lure hooked its flipper to its face." He shook his head and shrugged.

Barry wanted to shake Carl sometimes—so nonchalant. Apathetic, really. Manatees arrived almost weekly with lacerations and infirmities too gruesome to imagine: boat propeller strikes that sliced through tough hide like creamy butter, extreme emaciation from loss of seagrass, illness from toxic red tide algal blooms. And that young male with "FUCK YOU" etched on his back. Scumbag actually took a knife to him, for God's sake.

Barry shuddered. Nothing but evil, and all he could do was usher these astonishing creatures—so remarkable, so endangered, so trusting—back to their mutilation and slaughter. Powerless to do more. Powerless like always—the kid who didn't get a coveted toy for Christmas that his sister got instead. The scrawny teen who never gained respect from other kids. Bullied. Stymied in his career, frozen as assistant township manager, forever passed over by younger—taller—colleagues. Couldn't even manage to father offspring. Powerless against life's injustices. Just as he was no match now for the menacing rise of Deb's cantankerous independence.

Poseidon hardly resembled the mighty, hot-tempered Greek god of the sea. He was on the small side. Not yet fully grown, but almost. A teenager, hanging lethargically in the shallow water beneath the cypress trees at the quiet western edge of the springs, still confined to a holding pen reserved for recovering manatees.

Doctors at the zoo had removed the lure from his flipper and face, and the wounds were nearly healed. He was almost ready to be released into the main springs with the other manatees, free to venture into surrounding waterways. But Barry had rarely seen a rehabbed manatee so unresponsive, seemingly defeated. Most revived during their time here and quickly resumed life in the wider world, seemingly without fear of the dangers they might meet, without resentment or bitterness. But Poseidon had barely stirred since arriving.

Barry reached for his walkie-talkie. Carl should know. But his phone buzzed first. Deb.

"Hey," he growled.

"Oh good, I got you." Her voice sounded rushed, breathless.

"Everything okay?"

"Good news … I won a teacher's award."

Barry watched Poseidon. Neither moved.

"Did you hear me?"

"I did." Barry steeled himself. The morning air was already close and warm. "What award?"

"Michigan Teachers' Association … I'm Teacher of the Year!"

Perspiration formed on Barry's forehead. "Wow."

"Is this a bad time? You sound tired."

"No, just busy."

"Oh … I won't keep you." Deb paused. "I was hoping you'd come up for the ceremony… In three weeks."

Poseidon rose to the surface and drew in air through his bulbous snout, hovering before gliding slowly away, then circling back, suddenly coming to life. He repeated this several times.

"Maybe," Barry said.

"It'd mean a lot."

Poseidon circled faster, round and round, water churning. Barry felt dizzy. No, crazy. Furious. Like he was swimming in circles, too. Everything felt wrong.

"I'll try," he said, closing his eyes and massaging the back of his sweaty neck. Releasing tension, scattering annoyance, deflecting guilt. Yet another waymark on Deb's solo path to self-glory. Why should he feel guilty?

"I want to come," he said, struggling to sweeten his voice and make it sound true. "There's just a lot on my plate … Injured and sick manatees every day."

"Okay, we'll talk tonight." Deb's voice was hurt. "I love you."

Barry nodded without a word as if she were there to see his response. Then he jabbed the "End Call" button and shoved the phone in his pocket. His body trembled all over. Did Deb really expect him to drop everything and run to her side? When she wouldn't come here? It truly was outrageous—her lack of regard for his dreams and desires.

Poseidon slowly drifted back toward Barry, hanging again just below the water's surface, spiritless. From mad-crazy to calm in seconds. How did he do it? Barry turned and spit on the ground behind him, still shaking. Why did Deb's life always go her way? Always.

Barry popped the cap off his fourth Florida Cracker IPA, made by a local microbrewery. He loved the tongue-in-cheek name, flipping off the high and mighty. A real hoot. He downed half the bottle and dug into the Cheetos bag beside him on the narrow Airstream bed, staring at the rapid-fire montage of soundless images flashing on the muted TV—shiny people, gleaming sports cars, bounding tigers, toilet paper, jets, chocolate bars, you name it. It was nearly midnight.

His earlier call with Deb had ended quickly—parent meeting, book group, nothing more about her upcoming award ceremony. Barry didn't mention Poseidon either. Why should he? She was the one who'd started this whole rupture—still too fresh, even after three years, to fully replay in his mind.

Barry crunched the thought away and rubbed his gut, which had grown tubbier in the weeks since his arrival. No Deb to bug him about his health. Hell, maybe he'd swing by the Sweet Spot tomorrow, his one Saturday off a month, for mint fudge ripple ice cream heaped with a scoop of maple bourbon. Barry let out a belch. He'd pick up more microbrews, too, and maybe even some cigarettes. He'd quit those for Deb years ago, but what the hell. She'd sure be sorry for giving him his rope.

Barry cracked open another microbrew and took a long swig, savoring how it slid down his throat and smothered all feeling, like a manatee embraced in soothing waters. He was pleased with his plan—no harm in an occasional indulgence. He downed the rest of the bottle, waking at daybreak halfway off the bed, muted TV still on, empty IPA bottles cluttering the floor below him.

Three weeks later, at sundown, Barry found himself again at the western edge of the springs, watching Poseidon. He'd opened the gate to the main springs days ago, but Poseidon remained in the holding pen, listless as ever. The evening was muggy. Barry flashed to Deb in frigid Lansing, dressing to receive her award tonight. He'd forced himself to congratulate her that afternoon— texted a quick applause emoji as he wolfed down an Italian sub on break. Big clapping cartoon hands. A show of support. There in spirit. Deb promised to send pictures. What more could he do? Poseidon still hadn't recovered. They counted on him here.

Barry squatted by the water and dipped in his hand. Poseidon stirred.

"Why won't you heal?" he whispered. Someone should be hanged for this disgrace. And for Deb's treachery, too.

Poseidon surfaced briefly, giving a low, watery snort. Barry snorted, too. Hell, Deb didn't love him; it couldn't be clearer. He wasn't asking for much. Tropical warmth, saving manatees—these things moved him. Why couldn't she grant him this one wish?

Barry squeezed his eyes shut. He'd said as much that awful evening three years ago. Memories flooded his brain,, a mammoth deluge he'd struggled to blockade since then. Unstoppable.

"I've always gone along with everything you wanted," Deb said, a tear slipping down her cheek. "I just don't like Florida."

"But we planned it ... together ... you're saying you never meant it?" His voice sounded pleading, strangled.

"I thought I could go. I'm so sorry, Barry."

He clenched his fists, unable to look at her. "We were a team…"

"Barry, please." Deb came toward him. "Listen to me."

Barry backed away, pressure building inside his skull. "So everything you've ever done was to please me?" The words felt like jagged chunks in his throat. "Is that right?"

"Barry, no."

He sank to the sofa and stared at Deb. Her skin looked almost green in the dying light. Shadows cut lines across her face. This wasn't Deb. Not his Deb.

"I think I tried to make you happy," she said, sitting beside him.

"So you wouldn't leave."

"My God, Deb… What are you saying…?"

"I wanted this to work—us." She clutched his knee. "Not be like my parents. Create a better family. Then we couldn't …" Her voice almost disappeared. "I did what I thought would keep us together."

Barry couldn't speak, couldn't move.

She pressed closer. He could feel her heat. Damp, vaguely fetid. "Maybe I was also trying to make up for you never getting a fair shake," she whispered.

Barry flinched and shoved her hand off his knee. "You felt sorry for me?"

"No. Barry …." Deb scrubbed away tears.

"You still feel sorry for me … don't you!" Certainty overwhelmed Barry.

"No, Sweetie … I love you … I just forgot to make myself happy, too." Deb's face was unrecognizable. "I'm only asking for us to stay here. That's all. Please. For me."

At that moment, an emptiness filled Barry, so vast he was sure he'd never find his way through. Deb's true M.O. couldn't be clearer: She was no different from all the others. She felt superior and viewed him as hopeless, a charity case. She was done trying to help. She was looking out for herself now. Abandoning him, focused only on what pleased her.

Barry stared at Poseidon, then removed his boots and socks and waded into the water. Deb's every action since then was only further proof of his terrible realization that night. Not only did she not leave Michigan, but she also took up tennis, a pottery class, tai chi, lunches with friends, and a book group. She continued working, refusing to stop.

God knows Barry tried to applaud her growth, viewing it as something that would enhance his life, not leave him behind. But Deb's list of interests and demands seemed inexhaustible, each one another grotesque, unrelenting reminder of her aim to surpass him, outgrow him. His brain simply refused to accept any other interpretation.

Barry inched into the springs, water up to his knees, thoughts rumbling ominously like an approaching army. He could barely keep his balance. Deb was rejecting him. There was no denying it any longer. A rejection like no other. Leaving behind a bloody trail of flesh—his flesh—in her unwavering march toward the inevitable end.

*Please help me!* Barry heard the cry in his head. Or maybe out loud. A roar. Poseidon descended to the floor of the springs.

Barry roared again, animal agony. He'd show Deb, damn her. Burn everything to the ground. Divorce her. Leave her nothing. Nab someone younger, more adventurous. Fitter. Sad how Deb had let herself go. She'd probably die alone. If only… Barry slammed off the vision, but not before savoring its jolt of thrilling satisfaction.

He sank into the water to his chest, still clothed, heart pounding. Where did these thoughts come from? So overwhelming in their detail and persistence, out of his control: fantasies of revenge, rampaging down mountains into villages, pillaging, plundering, murdering.

Rage. A ghastly thicket inside him, too immense and almighty to dismantle—like dark energy in the universe. Even if Barry managed to push in and parse its individual strands, how would he withstand the obliterating gravitational pull of what he discovered, all the ugliness and anguish? How could he release it? There was simply too much.

Barry braced himself as a new revelation nearly sucked him underwater. My God, this great ball of ire wasn't new. He'd felt it all before, so many times. But the fury sparked by each affront wasn't unique to that incident, including Deb's many betrayals. Barry's outrage, he now realized, was generic, always there, waiting in dark corners to lunge at the next indignity and then the next. Same wrath, new offenses.

Tears dropped one by one. Deb's refusal to retire was simply the bullseye du jour for his perpetual umbrage. So was the plight of manatees. More targets would arrive, and then more. And on and on.

Barry slipped into the depths and went limp beside Poseidon. They watched one another, a deepwater dream of kinship, united in their shared ambivalence on the merits of a future. What if Barry never met someone new? Who would he talk to? No kids. No intimate friends. No Deb. What if he was the one who died alone?

Poseidon rose for air, then dropped again. His tiny eyes radiated wisdom. At least, that's how it seemed to Barry. Serenity spread across his odd and kindly face. What a relief to simply stop warring, to let go into nothingness.

Poseidon circled Barry slowly, grunting ruefully as if in a mournful song. Then he nudged him with his great whiskered snout, steering him through the dark water. Barry's body relaxed, roly-poly, comical, absurd, like Poseidon. He surrendered to the creature's tender navigation, buoyed by his ancient sea-god lullaby.

Sunrise colored the eastern sky when Barry woke at the edge of Wakunah Springs. Poseidon hung nearby, flippers gently stirring the water as if waving. Both of them still here. Not blissfully eradicated as Barry expected.

Poseidon turned finally and swam through the gate slowly back to life.

"Goodbye," Barry murmured. He dragged himself out of the water, dripping, and retrieved his boots and socks. Another loss, but somehow different. There was no time to dwell, though. Poseidon's departure needed to be reported. His healing. It would be a hectic day. Barry lingered, not quite ready. Rage rumbled deep in his belly, but not as forcefully as before, edges tinged with something softer.

Why were ancient gods so angry anyway? Forcing humans to cower and obey. What good did it ever do? Barry had swum with Poseidon, not mighty at all—unable to sustain anger. Not like the real Poseidon. Simply petrified. Frightened and wounded, powerless against humans, yet willing to forgive.

Perhaps angry gods weren't all that different. Pitiful and scared like Poseidon, but bolstered by a stubborn layer of rancor and combativeness. Like Barry. Not heroes to emulate but cautionary tales. Terrified of losing control and status, tempers masking fear of worthlessness, rage that might be transformed for more productive use.

Barry had seen it floating below rage with Poseidon, beneath tales he cherished, under grievances and pain, down to dread. Dread that he wasn't enough, an insignificant and useless man, alone. Impotent to pilot his own life, unworthy. The root of all anger. Poseidon had found the will to heal. He'd saved Barry, offering him the same chance. Summoning love. Real love. Transforming love. Barry had glimpsed it. The lightness and weight of love, life's shine. He could do better.

Barry wandered toward the park office, enveloped by birdsong. He was calm—perhaps just for now—alien but sweet. He loved himself here by the springs. He loved Deb. He did. He knew what healing required. Forgiveness for the man he'd been. Compassion for a new man finding his way. Candor and clarity with Deb—my God, she loved what she loved too, buried for too long. A laying of cards on the table—his and Deb's both—every humiliating fear, appalling thought, hurtful reverie, souls bared. Perhaps love could grow, a love big enough for all possibilities, compromise, and transformation. Poseidon flowed in those currents.

Barry swatted at a cloud of gnats. Rage reverberated again in the distance—a familiar path, easy. Love would require so much. Almost too much—the currents ran deep there but not beyond reach.

# PRICELESS
## By Gabrielle Gold

IN TONES OF BRIGHTNESS, the fields sang back.

Ariana caught the ripple in her hand, each chime a dancing ring of light in her mind. Sometimes she remembered the sensation of true light, in its millions of colors, but the memories faded in the presence of this otherworldly music.

The shimmering waves drew her towards the source, a trail of pulses leading back to the heart of it all.

"It's here," Ariana said, halting over a nearly imperceptible rise in the earth.

"Looks like everywhere else," the boy muttered. "But all right."

The grating of his shovel preceded a whiff of disturbed wet grass, a scent that darkened in quality with each thump of turned soil.

At last, the music swelled. Ariana let go of the breath she had not realized she was holding. Since she could not pinpoint the depth of her finds, eager prospectors had lost patience before, only to have another take their place in the same spot and emerge victorious.

A higher-pitched sound rang out, metallic and triumphant.

"I'll be damned!" The boy grunted, his feet shifting on the ground. A spray of dust tickled Ariana's nose as he scrabbled for the beacon she saw so clearly, but not with her eyes.

"I don't understand," he babbled. "How did you know it was here? There must be three pounds of silver!"

"I just know," Ariana said shyly.

"Great find!" Sister Madeline crowed. "There's an embossed bowl, a garnet necklace, two inlaid daggers, a—oh, this statuette's engraving is gorgeous."

"Wait until Pa sees this!" The boy jumped up, then turned to her and bowed, his clasped hands pressed against his forehead. "I don't know what to say...thank God for you, Sister. Thank God that you're here."

Heat flared at Ariana's collar. Even after four months of traveling from town to town, following the patchwork calls of riches below their feet, the stunned reverence given to her with each find left her floundering. She would never understand what the proper response to near-worship should be. Besides, she was no saint.

The boy did have reason to thank her, since she had solved his family's struggles with ailing goat herds in a single stroke. But he would never really know how much she cherished the gratitude of the poor. It was more priceless than any of her gleaming discoveries in the earth.

The song of the silver subsided on the way back to town, as it always did. Burial in the earth created every pattern of notes, like pressure on harp strings. When the pressure eased, the music dissipated into the background, an ephemeral mist.

They reached the inn before long, and Ariana felt for the edge of the low bed she was sharing with Madeline. Finding it, she yawned and proceeded to sprawl out on the pallet. Using her sense for precious metals took an unexplained toll. Madeline had no need for a luxurious afternoon nap, but Ariana had played her part for the day. The chance to make a difference, to give back to the common folk, was more than she had ever been able to do with her eyes.

She slid her arm under the pillow, hugging it close. If being blind meant gaining this strange vision, she almost wished it had happened sooner. Maybe her childhood would have been better spent.

When Ariana woke, she was uncertain how long her nap had been. Half-remembered dreams of her years in the cloister brushed the edge of her mind, and they rattled her more than she might have expected. Hesitantly, she slid off the bed and found her shoes and walking stick. Madeline would not be far.

Sure enough, the other Sister hailed her only two steps out the front door.

"Oh, good. I'm glad you got a bit more sleep in. Supper's underway at the tavern, though," Madeline said. "Let's go before they run out of fresh bread."

Ariana laughed. "Because that's the most important part." Her half-smile faded after a moment. "Maddie."

"...yes?" Madeline's tone shifted with the change in the air.

"I was thinking about the ravine."

Her friend exhaled slowly. "What about it?"

One year to the day after the fever stole her sight, Ariana had received her ethereal gift. Madeline believed what she told her then, in spite of the odds. Her sight had truly been replaced by visible music, prismatic as light through a crystal, that only she could perceive. Far-off but so clear, a beacon to guide them through her endless night. Following it had taken them into forbidden territory, past the borders of the abbey grounds and down into the narrow, stony valley where the river ran. But under the moon Ariana would never see again, Madeline led the way.

And they had unearthed a trove of wonders.

They had left the abbey within days of the find, laden with wealth and hope. Four months later, the afterglow of silver and gold had become a staunch companion, ready to change lives for the better wherever she went.

"What if there was more that we didn't find?"

Madeline hummed softly to herself. "Well, we won't know unless we go back."

"No chance," Ariana huffed.

"Then why worry about it?" Madeline said. "If we were meant to find it, we would have. God provides." She paused. "Oh, and you help."

Ariana could hear the infectious smile in her voice. "We made the right choice," she replied, more to herself than to Madeline. "I know we did."

"I'd certainly say so, based on the goatherder's reaction. He thinks you're sent straight from heaven."

"I know." Ariana linked her hands. "Certain people back home would have a different opinion."

"You're brooding." Madeline nudged her lightly. "Let's get some supper. You always get cranky when you're hungry."

"Oh, fine." The warmth of her friend's hand guiding her lifted some of the weight from her shoulders.

They left an hour later, their bellies pleasantly full. Halfway back to the inn, Madeline halted quite suddenly and gripped Ariana's hand.

"Praise God. We've found you at last."

Ariana knew the speaker all too well.

"Abbess," Madeline said tightly. "What brings you so far from home?"

"I would ask the same of you, but I have some idea," the Abbess said, the consonants in her speech forming harsh edges. "Never before have I seen runaways. We've only treated you well." She stopped, and Ariana wondered which one of them was on the receiving end of her iron-tipped gaze. "And now, you'll come back with me."

"No," Ariana said flatly. Madeline's swift intake of breath was a warning, but she ignored it. "I'm happy on the road. I can help the common folk here. I'm not going back."

"You are a Sister, Ariana. Your duty is to God, and to our abbey's benefactors," the Abbess said. "Let those who distribute charity and care for the sick do their good work. You have a different calling. A higher purpose."

Panic welled in Ariana's throat. How much did the Abbess

know? She had always lauded her scribal work, but never in such a lofty, ecstatic tone.

"You should be grateful," the Abbess said, sudden frost returning to her voice. Ariana almost shivered at the chill between them. "I'm giving you a second chance to do what God intended for you." Her rigid shoes struck the packed dirt path as she strode forward, a reprimand in each step.

"That's—" Madeline choked back anything else.

"She found this, didn't she? The boy's father surrendered it willingly once I explained. Did you know what it is, Sister?"

"What do you mean?" Madeline said. "It's a statuette. I can't read the engraving. Maybe he was a noble?"

The Abbess scoffed. "You forget your studies."

Something clicked, like a latch being released. Sweat blossomed on the back of Ariana's neck. The statuette was a container. Hopefully, there was just more silver inside, or perhaps a secret message from a lover.

The only other option was impossible.

Madeline stopped breathing. Then she began to cry.

Ariana's arms went slack. "It's a relic, isn't it," she whispered.

"The finger of Saint Kerrigan," the Abbess intoned.

Saint Kerrigan, who led the king to victory after his unjust exile. Who heralded the golden age of Royal Prophets.

What did God intend for her, after all?

The Abbess had no such uncertainties about Ariana's fate. As the woman outlined her future with grand, sweeping gestures, Ariana grew numb. She heard the words but could not absorb them through the fog descending around her.

That haze only broke once they were shunted back into the inn and locked inside, away from gawking onlookers and demanding visions. But the modest building had become their temporary prison, the Abbess' guards stationed at the door.

"I don't know what to do," Madeline sobbed, the sound muffled by her handkerchief. "I want you to be happy, Ari. I want that more than anything. But is this a sign?"

In that moment, the situation crystallized. If she had any gratitude left, Ariana would have appreciated the lack of other travelers in the inn.

"It's a sign," Ariana snapped. "A sign that the Abbess is not in the service of God. Otherwise, she would leave us in peace to be what we're meant to be. I'm not hurting anyone. *This* is my calling, not playing relic-hunter." After centuries of sending their sons and daughters into God's service, little could disentangle the nobility from the church as an establishment. Saint Kerrigan had only tightened the bond between church and crown. The Abbess was convinced that someone with the ability to locate holy relics would inevitably serve the royal cathedral, increasing its glory and prestige. All in the supposed name of the divine.

"You've almost broken your ankle three times already," Madeline wailed. Ariana could hear her walking in circles, pacing what small bit of floor space was not occupied by other beds. "The royal guards would be much better guides for you on the road than I ever could. I know this isn't what you want. But you didn't want to be blind, either..."

"Maddie!" Ariana shouted. She rose to her feet so fast she almost caught her shoes on the hem of her robes. "Do you think this is about you?! You've been my guide, my friend, my light in the dark. You believed me when I said something crazy that night, and I love you for it." Her voice cracked. "Don't turn back on me now."

Madeline only continued sniffling.

With great effort, Ariana lowered her voice to a soft growl. "We can still run. Isn't there a large window in the corner? I bet it's not guarded. The Abbess thinks you're broken, but I don't believe it." Ariana grasped the air, searching for the other Sister's shoulder, but it eluded her. "I can't do this without you."

"I don't know," Madeline said. "I think—I think—" She blew her nose.

The poor woman was probably a snotty mess, but Ariana refused to give up. "Please."

After a long silence, Madeline finally whispered back.

"I think we should go to sleep."

They lay down, facing away from each other. Ariana muffled her tears in the woolen covers. Everything seemed so clear, but there was nothing left to say.

Ariana stirred as Madeline shook her gently. The cool temperature meant night must have fallen hours ago.

"I'm sorry," Ariana mumbled, her head still heavy with lingering nightmares. She remembered they had an argument, at least. "For yelling at you." What was it about?

The Abbess.

"No, I'm sorry," Madeline turned over and took her hand. "I haven't slept much. But I thought it over again. You're right."

Ariana started fully awake. Madeline thought she was right? That meant…

A laugh, weak from disbelief, almost bubbled out of her before she caught herself.

"Blessed are the humble, the faithful, and the poor. They will reap what they have earned by living rightly," Madeline quoted. "If you're God's answer for the poor, I support that. You shouldn't have to spend your life searching for lost treasures that the needy will never see."

Ariana threw her arms around Madeline. As her friend hugged her back, tears slid down her cheek. If only she could see Madeline smile one more time.

In a quiet but inelegant fashion, they squeezed through the corner window, packs and all. As suspected, the Abbess thought Madeline sufficiently cowed into obedience and had been satisfied with her watchmen at the entrance. Sacred though that statuette might be, it could not contain their future.

They left the town behind, avoiding the main road. No one saw them, and no one stopped them. She would be on the run for some time, but with Madeline beside her, aligned in purpose, she had never felt so free.

Only a few pilgrims lingered at the mouth of the sacred cave after most had already retired for the evening. Laypeople and clergy of all sorts came to pray and give thanks at this site, where the rich and poor rubbed shoulders during the peak of travel season. Most peasants were too occupied by tilling and sowing crops at this time of year, so the crowd was thinner than it could have been.

Having sworn a vow of poverty, Sister Daphne was forbidden to keep more wealth on her person than what she required for her journey. Her Order's balance of ideals and actions had stood the test of time: poverty was holy, and so was taking steps to achieve their mission. To that end, those who made the pilgrimage here were permitted the coin they needed for provisions and a suitable offering—but no more.

Past precedent dictated what constituted a 'suitable offering' from acolyte pilgrims, but Daphne questioned what their patron saint would have really wanted. They were tasked with caring for those in low places, and saints were in the highest place of all. Her doubt had spurred her to defy tradition.

Nodding once to herself, Daphne placed the amulet she brought with the other offerings. The flimsy tin pendant seemed sullenly mundane amongst the glistening array of bronze and silver. One worshiper had been extravagant enough to leave a slim vessel of gold.

As she withdrew her hand, she pretended not to hear the judgmental whispers off to her left. That woman could shove her velvet-trimmed cloak where the sun didn't shine.

"May I reap what I have earned by living rightly," she mouthed, rising to her feet. She smoothed back the wispy hair tugged from her cowl by the spring breeze. Tomorrow, she would start for home.

The local church provided pilgrims with shelter during their stay, so the beds were full, if not bursting as they would be during the summer months. Still, it was better to be cramped and warm. The nights could get bitter in the mountains.

Daphne wound her way around the maze of cots and sleeping forms to the bed she was sharing with a lanky girl who introduced herself only as 'Berta'. Before crawling beneath the free corner of wool blanket, she tugged it down to cover the young woman's feet.

In the morning, she bid a silent goodbye to the resting place of Saint Ariana, founder of Daphne's Order—the Holy Wanderers.

Her journey home was uneventful for weeks, which was just fine. Daphne welcomed a future newly blessed by God's beloved. She stared into the distance one evening, content to watch the tree branches and their newborn leaves sway before darkness hid them away. This was what peace felt like. She had hopes for more of the same.

Until the next morning, when the fields sang back.

# IN THE SHADOW'S EDGE
## By Stephen Woodfall

SHADOWS NEVER TOLD LIES. For those with the skill to spot it, the truth was laid bare within the Element of Shadow, in the shifting of its penumbra.

Old Sketta eyed the prospective customer with dismay as he stumbled into her ratty tent at dusk, stinking of cheap mead in particular and the caravansary in general. His boots were still soiled with whatever he had been mucking all day, his old garments dirty and tattered. From under a mop of grimy hair, he swung his gaze around the inside of the tent as if uncertain how he had arrived there.

But when his gaze locked onto hers, he said, "You the *akamaja*?"

Remaining in her chair, Old Sketta narrowed her eyes on the man. It was rare that a simple laborer could afford her services, and she hated the idea of having to spend several bothersome minutes saying *no* a dozen different ways before he left.

"They said you was." He pointed over his shoulder lazily with a thumb. "Old Sketta, they said. I need a reading."

The man's face was a blank page. Whatever personality he

may have possessed, nothing of it showed in his expression. She stared a moment longer, then said, "You do, do you?"

"Yeah, I…" A light dawned in his eye; clearly, he had come to understand at least part of her hesitation. His hand disappeared into a pocket and came out flashing silver. "I can pay."

Old Sketta's eyebrows shot up. "It appears you can." Straightaway her eyebrows went back down. "Laborers don't usually carry that much coin. Is that something I should be concerned about?"

The man's puzzlement looked genuine. "No. No, nothing to be concerned about. Don't… Just don't waste the money, that's all. So, are you the *akamaja*? Will you read, or what?"

She regarded him coolly. "What's your name?"

"Ossek."

Of course. One of the most common names in the country. Everyone knew three Osseks at least.

"Yes, Ossek, I am Old Sketta." She drew in a long breath and brushed a twisting silver lock of hair aside. "Close the tent flap, and we'll get the fire going."

She pushed her creaking, spindly frame up out of her favorite chair, and added several chunks of cedar to the stout iron brazier standing in the center of the tent.

Like herself, her tent was well worn. It was everywhere frayed and stained with the soot of countless fires, but it had long suited her exacting needs. It had the proper shape and size and could ventilate smoke through holes up high while the flaps were all closed—a crucial feature for an *akamaja*. Despite its poor state, it was more convenient to keep than to replace.

She said, "It'll take a few minutes before the fire is burning right. Normally, I charge three *kaseers*..."

"Got that," said Ossek. "Have it right here." An upturned palm with three coins thrust uncomfortably close to her face.

"Yes, very well." She snatched the silver and then moved away before catching another whiff. She'd have to remember to toss a little incense into the flames next chance she got.

Coughing lightly, Old Sketta circled the fire's perimeter to retrieve her purposely-cut-down, extra-low stool.

"Now then," she said. "What sort of reading is it you want? Name the *kamaj*."

"Enchantment," said Ossek. "Need to know if some damn enchantment's been put on me."

Old Sketta set the stool down next to the brazier as the flames edged higher.

"Yes, enchantment. I can read that *kamaj*." A few years ago, she would have added a mysterious-sounding cackle, but she had since grown weary of putting on such an act. These days, her reputation more than sufficed to keep her in business. And besides, much of the practice wasn't an act at all, no matter how strange it appeared to newcomers. "And what makes you think you've been enchanted?"

"Do you really need to know that to read me? What do you care, anyway? I've paid, haven't I?"

The light in the tent had grown brighter, yet Old Sketta had trouble seeing her customer clearly. Who was this laborer, this Ossek? It was an odd thing, his wanting an enchantment reading.

Who would go to the trouble of putting that kind of sorcery on such a nobody? And why would that nobody spend what must be a several month's salary to find out if he'd been enchanted?

She peered at him openly.

Ossek's vacant stare yielded nothing useful. His clothing spoke only of toilsome drudgery. His casual demeanor rebuffed inquiry.

It was all very curious, but the lout was right—he had paid and it was none of her business.

"Oh, of course. I'm just a curious old woman. You're right, it's not important. But I can help you. You know, enchantment is not the only *kamaj* I can read."

Ossek stood where he was and said nothing.

"Indeed," she continued, attempting to ply him with levity. "Most *akamaji* know only two, maybe three, types of readings at most. But," she thrust a finger in the air to emphasize her point, "Old Sketta knows them all! There is no *kamaj* I have not learned."

"Enchantment," said Ossek. "Just enchantment, nothing more."

"Of course. The fire's nearly ready. Won't you take a seat?" She gestured toward the shortened stool.

Ossek moved over to the stool with an almost solemn, ceremonious air, and sat down. He cleared his throat and said, "Known about you for some time now, you know."

"You don't say? Well it's not too surprising. I'm nearly famous around here—the only *akamaja* between Nhurrain and Vinoora."

Old Sketta trundled over to one side of the tent just behind Ossek. Reaching up, she unfastened a broad swath of tent fabric, letting it unfurl nearly to the floor. A long dowel attached to the lower edge kept the cloth from waving or bunching.

Upon the fabric's flat, even surface, Ossek's shadow, cast by the fire, appeared in stark detail, almost as if a third person had joined them.

Old Sketta made her way back to the brazier to get a look at it.

"Was my brother," said Ossek.

She blinked. "Your brother? What about your brother?"

"Came to you for a reading some time ago."

"Is that so?" Old Sketta allowed herself a crooked smile. "Thus you learned of my prodigious talent, and have since sought me out." Over half her patrons had come to her in a similar manner. Word of her *akamaja* skills had long run up and down the great Nhurrain River.

Ossek lowered his head and four feet behind him his dark counterpart made the exact same motion.

Old Sketta took a step toward the tent-flap, peering at the solid black shadow. The leaping tongues of the firelight made the outline flicker faintly, casting dark grey echoes of itself in fleeting moments.

The shifting penumbra. A prime feature of the Element of Shadow.

Here it was that the truth could be seen, in a shadow cast from firelight. Candles, lamps, sorcerous illumination, the sun—no other kind of light revealed a penumbra that might be read. Only a proper-sized fire could do that.

"Happened last year," said Ossek. His gruff voice took on a dirge-like quality. "Ma brought him to you. Asked for a reading for him."

"It happens that way a lot," she said distractedly.

The shadow was wrong somehow. Old Sketta took another step forward.

Its penumbra was too narrow. The flashes of dark grey shadow should have been an inch wide. Yet they were barely a third of that. The signs of the *kamaj* she sought took place right along the sharpest edge of the shadow. They were difficult to see under normal circumstances, but in this case they were impossible. She squinted but it made little difference.

Ossek said, "The *kamaj* she asked you to look for was possession."

That got her attention. Possession was rare. In her life, she'd done that reading no more than five or six times. It could be dangerous, and it was never pleasant.

To cover her perturbation, she said, "Scoot toward the fire a couple of inches, would you dear? Seems I placed the stool in the wrong spot."

With a grunt, the man complied, his dark double mimicking the brutish movements.

When he had settled himself again, Old Sketta peered once more at the shadow on the tent-flap. The hunkered down shape had grown a little larger, as intended, and yet the penumbra remained frustratingly narrow.

*Last year* he had said. A memory struck the center of her mind like the clap of a thunderbolt on a sunny summer day.

The distraught mother had come to her with her stricken son. Old Sketta did a reading on him and found the young man had indeed been compromised by a malevolent entity. The discovery frightened Old Sketta immensely, had shaken her brittle bones. What happened after was a blur, but she knew that some authorities took the lad away with the hysterical mother at their heels. He had been hanged within the hour.

An *akamaja's* work often involved dealing with unpleasant news, or disturbing circumstances. But possessions were far more perilous. If the person whom the entity had possessed was put to death swiftly enough, the entity would not survive as well. However, if it *could* latch onto someone else in time, someone nearby, the thing's vengeance would know no bounds.

The fire popped and spluttered, jarring Old Sketta's mind back to the present.

Studying the firelight shade again, she realized what she'd missed.

Old Sketta caught her breath.

Seeking signs of enchantment, she had missed the other sign. The sign of possession. A thin, dark line along the edge—not merely black, but a deep, vast emptiness, like the space between the stars. Fascination and horror arose in her in the same instant.

Shadows never told lies.

In the Element of Shadow, the truth had been laid bare in its penumbra once more.

Somehow, beyond all likelihood, that entity had survived.

Time slowed to an agonizing crawl while Ossek's shadow stood up. As Old Sketta's heart quailed the living shade expanded, filling the entire tent flap with deep darkness.

The darkness became an icy void, and the void flooded outward, snuffing out the fire and Old Sketta's gasp.

# SAVIOR COMPLEX
## By Autumn Shah

ELIANA WALKED THE SEAWALL, checking for signs of damage to the concrete and wood structure after last night's violent waves. In her satchel, she carried salvaged upholstery thread and a large needle to repair any ripped sandbags. Her ears were attuned to any change in the sound of the water's constant lapping, but still, she avoided turning her back to the wide expanse. Sudden, powerful waves, and the tremors that caused them, were becoming more frequent— a constant threat to the protective walls that Eliana and the people of the zone so diligently tended.

Gazing across the water, she was struck by a sense of formidable allure and a deep, quaking fear that had been part of her even before the Global Seismic Apocalypse that had swept her family from her grasp almost three years ago.

Six square miles of livable space remained of Ohio. The now watery landscape before her had once been a network of roads with manicured trees, strip malls, a boutique grocery store, and the various office buildings of a micropolitan city. A little further in the distance, she could see the submerged freeway overpass that had once arched high above the main road. Now, it served as a natural breakwater to the wall they had built. It was then, among the undulating shapes of the waves, that she saw an object bobbing along the horizon.

She ran as best she could across the rocks and debris. Wrestling open the rusted door that gave access to her quadrant, she stepped over the lip and fought it closed again. She raced up the outdoor stairway of Hi-Point Church that led straight to the roof and the catwalk that had been added when it was decided the obnoxiously large, neon-lit cross would make a perfect "lighthouse."

Sure enough, the faraway shape was a boat.

She headed to Sloan Hall, where she knew the always unflappable council leader, Joyce, would already be up and working on the day's shower passes or debris allocation. As soon as Eliana veered off Sandusky Avenue, she caught up with Mira, who was obviously on her way to her breakfast shift. Mira and her teenage daughters, Zaynab and Rania, were the closest thing to family Eliana had.

"Hey, Mira, good morning," Eliana said, panting.

"Good morning! Where are you off to so early?"

"I was out checking the wall, and I saw a boat."

"Did you call it in?" Mira asked.

Eliana patted her hip where a walkie-talkie rested beneath her parka. "Yeah."

"Do you think it's one of the boats we're expecting?"

"I hope so. I'm sure Les knows by now," Eliana said.

Les, a sweet, elderly man with a glorious white beard, was their radioman. He had been in contact with a man named Griffin, who was originally from the colony and was now returning.

She'd heard his name often. His regular radio contact over the past twenty-two months had kept them apprised of the viability of other zones. But to Eliana, he was as mythic as his namesake, an elusive creature over the radio waves she wasn't sure truly existed.

"Well, let me know what you find out," Mira said.

Soon enough, everyone on Coastal Persistence Colony 4 would know.

For the life of her, Eliana could not put a face to the name. Griffin had apparently left the zone five months after the GSA, at a time when everyone was in the raw stages of shock and grief. The exhaustion of daily survival and the trauma of the changed world blurred those months out of her memory.

Griffin's travels and regular messages had prompted clusters of migration—not just from CPC4, but from colonies all over—to larger, and therefore safer and more sustainable landmasses. Quebec was a popular destination for Midwesterners who didn't trust the clannish folk of Appalachia. Or, more likely, didn't want to risk a wave pushing them off course and missing one of the islands of the Appalachian Archipelago.

A new migration westward began when sea levels rose above what trackers estimated was 400m. The Coastal Persistence Province of the Great Plains was where CPC4 would evacuate.

As they watched the boat approach, Les filled her in on the disappointing and possibly catastrophic news that the other two boats Griffin was traveling with had been separated during the last set of waves.

"A class III isn't going to fit as many as a Fenner & Hood cruiser," Les told her. He had been a general foreman in the Before with no experience with boats, but his curiosity and questions had made him an expert on the make, model, and specification of all types of seacraft.

Just then, Joyce ducked through the seawall door. "Good morning!" she called.

Keith, an alpha male who acted like he should be head of the council, followed.

Joyce was like the big sister Eliana never had, even though Joyce was younger. It could be that Joyce was so much taller and broader or that she was the wiser, more put-together of the two.

They watched as the port side was lined up to the concrete dock, and Eliana smiled at the boat's clever name, *Savior Complex*. When it was aligned properly, the man emerged from the cockpit and threw the mooring to Keith who was at the ready.

"Morning!" the man called out before disappearing to the starboard side.

He reemerged carrying two burlap sacks, which he tossed

overboard.

"I couldn't come back empty-handed after all this time," he said of the bags before disappearing again.

Les and Joyce both grabbed a sack. Griffin emerged with a pack on his back and a bundle of cloth in his arms. Eliana could see he would have to drop the cloth or hand it over before going down the ladder, so she stepped forward and climbed a rung to reach him.

"Careful," he said.

Eliana held her arms out. As soon as she did, she felt a squirming body. She stepped backward onto the dock and adjusted the patched fabric until it stopped squirming. A sour smell emanated from the bundle.

The man was in front of her now, tall and gaunt, all angles.

"I'm Griffin," he said as he untangled a corner of the cloth to reveal the salt-and-pepper muzzle of a dog. "This one's a little seasick."

"Aw, poor thing," Joyce said, leaning over Eliana's shoulder. And to Griffin, "Welcome back."

"Thanks," he said in a soft, raspy voice.

"Yeah, it's been a few," Keith said. "Shall we?" He led the way off the dock.

Eliana couldn't believe she held a dog in her arms. She felt butterflies in her chest and an instant possessiveness as if only she could protect this vulnerable creature.

"Her name is Captain," Griffin said.

Eliana smiled at him and fought tears of gratitude that tingled her nose.

"Perfect for a seasick dog," Keith said wryly.

"Those were some rough waves out there last night, I bet," Les said, closing the seawall door behind them. "They slammed our south side pretty good. Swallowed up more of the floodplains.".

"Yeah, I was green around the gills myself," Griffin said.

"Do you think there's much hope for the other two boats?" Joyce asked. "Have you had any contact with them?"

"No contact still. But Aidan and Darmesh are skilled on the water. I have my hopes we'll hear from them soon."

They passed the hangar where workers repaired boats and outfitted pontoons for the rougher waters than those of Indian Lake nearby, all in preparation for an exodus that was the focus of most of their productivity these days, and the constant topic of conversation.

Eliana did not mind all the preparations; it kept her busy and useful. But the constant talk of hull fittings, bilge pumps, currents, and emergency procedures settled on her chest, heavy and suffocating, like the weight of an anchor pulling her under.

"You must be exhausted," Eliana said to him.

"We'll get you set up at the commons with some food and a cot," Joyce offered.

"And some fresh water and rosemary for a spit bath," Les said, grimacing and pinching his nose.

"I'm glad someone said something!" said Keith, laughing.

"That would be great. Maybe while I do that, someone could brew some coffee?"

"We haven't had coffee here since—Wait! Did you bring

*coffee*?" Joyce spun to look at him.

Griffin grinned.

"I bow to you most humbly," she said, dipping her head.

"It's not much. Hopefully, you have more tea drinkers."

"Eliana here is our representative tea drinker."

"Eliana," Griffin said, almost as a question, turning slightly toward her. "Nice to meet you." He stuck his hand out, and she extricated her own from the bundle. His skin was cool and rough, and while he may have grasped her hand a little longer than usual, she found she didn't want to let go.

"The only good thing about tea," Keith said, "is that you can brew anything together, and it still tastes like dirt water."

"You just haven't had the right cup of tea," Eliana said, hoping he didn't take that as an offer.

"I think it's just the inside of your mouth," Joyce said.

"Ha-ha," Keith retorted.

"Do you want me to look after Captain while you rest?" Eliana asked Griffin.

He reached over and scratched behind the dog's ear.

"I can feed her some rice and scrambled egg to settle her stomach," she offered.

"You wouldn't mind?"

She nuzzled the dog's head in answer.

When they reached Sloan Hall, Les handed the sack over to Keith and continued to his radio room while Joyce and Keith took Griffin in.

Eliana headed to the cooking area, buoyed by a sense of

devotion that she wasn't sure came from the creature in her arms or the man who had finally ceased to be a myth.

Eliana stayed to help Mira clean up the second dinner seating, along with two other young men assigned. Afterward, they lit up the fire pit outside, and soon, Zaynab, Rania, and several others joined them. Captain had eaten and regained her land legs. She chased after Farah's son until the little boy's bedtime.

"Zee, come on!" Rania called to her sister.

Around and around, zigzagging back and forth, Captain chased the girls.

Mira beamed. "It's not often you get to see this."

"What, the dog?"

"Yes, but also the girls. Look at them. They're playing. Having *fun*. Not in survival mode," Mira said. "If you leave with us, you'll see this all the time."

Eliana groaned. Someone was always trying to convince her of the benefits of traveling across unpredictable waters with the many dangers above and below threatening to trap, drown, or suffocate.

"You know I won't step foot on a boat that's leaving the dock. No way," she said.

"I know, I know. But you have to think of the end result."

"You'd have to drug me and drag me," Eliana said.

"That's an idea." Mira poked at the fire. "Girls, let's go. We have to be up early." She turned to Eliana again; "I don't know how, or why, but somehow I feel it's in God's plans for us to all be together." The younger woman put an arm around Eliana and squeezed her in.

That night, Eliana curled up around Captain. Griffin had slept through dinner and Eliana was happy to keep Captain with her. She couldn't help comparing her state of mind now with that of last night; how she had sat in the sanctuary of Hi-Point, its cavernous ceiling belying the intimacy of the space. She had stared into the darkness until it morphed into undulating shapes and merged with the sound of the battering waves outside that were sure to envelop her someday. She had imagined yielding to her lifelong fear of water, plagued no more by the constant lapping that sometimes drowned out her thoughts, afraid no longer of the infinite darkness surrounding her.

Maybe this six-week shift as lighthouse watch wasn't good for her after all. She had looked forward to the prospect of living away from the small college's close quarters where the colony survivors made their homes. It was the center of their new life. But here, she had had too many nights where the tranquility allowed her to visit her grief and the fear of what she could never escape.

Tonight, the empty expanse of dread seemed just a little farther away. She wasn't sure if it was the miniature, grizzled mutt lightly snoring beside her, or the grizzled man who had brought her here, that caused the whirlpool of emotions she barely recognized.

Eliana awoke to Captain standing at the door staring her down.

"You need to go out, peanut?" She got up from her cot and slipped her shoes on. Through the window, the sun's glow shone below the horizon. She grabbed her daypack and carried Captain downstairs.

Under the hooded morning sky, the water sounded like it was right beside her, jiggling the lock, trying to find a way in. Hi-Point Church was the closest structure to the wall. Other than the smallholder farms further east, the church was the farthest structure from the college—a ten-minute walk, as the crow flies.

"Come on, girl," Eliana called to Captain. She wondered if Griffin was awake yet. Was it a decent hour to wake him? He probably missed his dog.

Eliana's steps were quick with excitement as she and Captain walked the trodden path through the grass and into the trees, Captain zigzagging slightly ahead.

When they reached the north solar grid that used to be the parking lot, she picked the dog up and carried her, heading into Sloan Hall. Zaynab, Mira's older daughter, and Rania would be leaving for their shifts soon, and Eliana hoped to surprise them with a 'good morning' visit from Captain. At seventeen, Zaynab was one of the best solar grid engineers they had. Rania worked shifts in the field and at the desalination station.

Zaynab saw Eliana first through the foyer window. "Hi, Auntie!" she waved.

Eliana waved back, and Captain squirmed to escape her arms. She put the dog down to find her way around the glass wall to where Zaynab was opening the door to their rooms.

"Oh, my goodness! You cutie," Zaynab said when Captain barrelled into her.

"Is that Captain?" Rania called out.

"Any news of the other boats?" Zaynab asked.

Eliana fished the walkie-talkie out of her pack to make sure it was on. "Apparently not," she said.

Rania appeared and bent down to rub Captain's belly.

Just then, Captain gave a start and bolted off behind them down the hall.

Griffin strode towards them.

"That's the man from the boat?" Zaynab asked.

"Yep."

Griffin looked up from his kneeling position, rubbing Captain's belly. "Thank you for taking care of her." He stood up. "It looks like we both got the rest we needed."

"It was my pleasure," Eliana said. "I don't know if you ever met them, but this is Zaynab and Rania. If you've been to breakfast already, you may have seen Mira, their mother."

"It's very nice to meet you both." Captain was jumping at his legs, so he bent down to pick her up. "I haven't been to breakfast yet, but I'm famished," he said.

"That's where we're all headed," Eliana said.

The four of them walked the corridor. Captain tilted towards Eliana and pawed at the air with a free leg. Eliana caressed the top of the dog's head.

"I think Auntie's in love," Rania said from behind.

Griffin said, "What's not to love?"

Eliana's chest bloomed red, realizing, belatedly, that they were referring to her

obvious affection for the dog. Zaynab caught her look, let out a snort, and playfully pushed Rania into the wall.

In the dining hall, they grabbed plates and stood in the mess line, Eliana attempting to look interested in anything but Griffin.

They chose a table together, but instead of sitting, Zaynab told Rania, "We're taking it to go." Giggling and whispering, they left together, much to Eliana's embarrassment.

After breakfast, Griffin went to the hangar to help with the boats while Eliana went to her shift at the food preservation bunker. As she canned plums and packaged dehydrated carrots, she thought about Griffin manipulating bolts and braiding nylon into ropes. She pictured the tendrils of hair that curled around his ears, which brought to mind her husband and how she had cut his hair for all those months during the COVID pandemic, four years before the GSA. The memory struck her with guilt.

Griffin and Captain had infused the cafeteria with a levity that had been absent for months. Anytime someone returned, or a new face arrived, there was excitement, but Captain's enthusiasm and affection for everyone was infectious. Griffin also endeared himself, exclaiming how much Robert's twin boys had grown and asking Farrah about her pregnancy. He also listened intently to Rania as they stood in line, and she explained her process of making face cream out of snail slime.

"Life is so much more pleasant with hydrated skin and minimized pores," he had said.

Eliana wondered if he, too, had once been a parent.

Now, in the close space of the bunker, the inside of her nose stung from the strong vapor of vinegar, and she wondered how long she had been at this. Not long enough, but she was antsy, so she finished her batch, cleaned up her space, and left.

She headed northeast to the corn and winter oat fields. She wondered how many people would be here in a few weeks when the crops needed harvesting. Perhaps it would just be her and the handful of others who planned to stay. She drifted into the rows of corn and imagined that day when the evacuation would be complete, and she remained. She had contemplated the eventuality many times, wondering if she could bring herself to board a boat and set off for a destination across a frightening abyss.

A handful of others were choosing to stay for various reasons: old age, disabilities, fear of the unknown. Some insisted they would 'pray it out,' while others were determined to go down with the land that generations of their families had tended. They were mostly people Eliana and Mira referred to as homesteaders; they grew, raised, and made most of their own food, sharing the remainder with the community. She supposed she would be reliant on them and would have to make more of an effort at friendship than she had.

Inside this half-acre cocoon of corn stalks, she could forget that she was closely surrounded by water. She imagined she was already alone, the only one left on CPC4. Usually, this silly game left her wanting to run back to Sloan Hall, Hi-Point Church, or wherever Zaynab and Rania might be to hug them and tell them how much they had healed her and helped her survive those hardest months.

Today, though, thinking of Griffin, she felt a stirring of something new. It felt like hope.

She left the fields and meandered toward the hangar. Maybe he would be outside; maybe Captain would catch her scent on the breeze. How silly she felt, hanging around with no good excuse to go inside.

She turned to go, then heard the voices at the hangar's entrance and quickened her step so she wasn't caught loitering around like a girl with a silly crush.

"El!"

No one had called her El except for her younger brother. She turned and saw Griffin waving at her and Captain springing toward her, tongue lolling out.

"How were the carrots doing?" Griffin asked.

"Uh, fine," she responded.

"That's good. Carrots are easy to deal with, huh? They don't usually carrot all."

Eliana laughed, shaking her head. He had definitely been a dad.

As they reached the middle of campus, they sensed a commotion. And then Eliana's walkie-talkie crackled.

"*Moaning Lisa* inbound. Repeat, *Moaning Lisa* inbound." They could hear the excitement in Les' voice.

"Twenty minutes to visual," Les said.

"That means they could potentially reach dock in under an hour, depending on how fast he's going," Griffin said. "Shall we head back the way we came?"

Eliana would have loved to remain in his company, but she was suddenly beset by a host of confounding emotions: the past, the present, and even her future colliding in a maelstrom she couldn't harness.

That night, the sky was velvet black, displaying layers upon layers of stars. Dinner was a lively event with the newcomers Aidan and his girlfriend Odessa telling the story of their days on the water, floating and sailing, floating and sailing with no communication, and rationing their food and water.

There was a lot of informal talk about the evacuation, the route they would take, the number of boats, the number of people, and how many they could safely fit. Ideas circulated about how to decide who got to go first and how long it would feasibly take for the boats to return for more.

Eliana stood to leave, the anchor weighing on her chest again. She meant to slip away, but Griffin drew up beside her.

"I think it's safer if I walk you home."

"Safer for you, or for me?" she asked.

"Me. Of course," he said. "See that lady over there?" He pointed to Thandie, a 77-year-old former yoga instructor with still-lean, tattooed arms. "She's had her eye on me all night."

"Oh my gosh." Eliana laughed, swatting his arm.

He rubbed his arm, then held it out to her. She took it, and a peculiar thrill washed over her.

Captain trotted and sniffed the ground ahead of them, already familiar with the path. For the first time, Eliana wished that Hi-Point Church was more of a walk. The flashlight beams bounced ahead of them, their silence a warm blanket against the damp night air.

Griffin broke the silence and said, "I get the feeling you don't trust I'll get us there safely."

"I—it's not that."

"I've been ferrying people from one colony to another for over a year. I've been to the CPP at least three times from closer colonies, but…".

She stopped and unsnaked her arm.

"We're here," Eliana said.

He searched her face, seeming to be unsure what to say.

"I feel like I need to walk you back now," Eliana said. "Thandie might be hiding in wait for you."

"Hmm, you're right. Maybe I should just stay here…" His hand grazed hers, and she entwined her fingers in his.

He leaned down and said, "Do you remember what a 'nightcap' is?"

She couldn't wait any longer. She tugged him in under the dark portico, where their flashlights gleamed and twinkled on the ceiling, and then led him up the stairs, her whole body effervescent with desire.

Old World Eliana would be horrified, inviting a man she barely knew to her bed. But that Eliana was younger and more cautious, and that world had its societal mores that she heedlessly conformed to. Now, she pulled him in as if the world would end tomorrow.

They lay on her mattress, basking in the glow of the giant, blue-white light of the cross outside the window. Captain lay in a corner on Griffin's side of the mattress.

"It's probably going to be some kind of lottery system we use to decide who goes this round."

She nuzzled into his neck, hoping to avoid serious talk.

"Are you worried about not being picked?" he continued.

"No."

"Why?"

"I'm not going."

"Huh," he grunted, running his fingers along her back. He was silent for a few moments and then, "Well, if you're going to stay here, I recommend getting some curtains." He laughed and held a hand to shade his eyes.

Eliana was helping Zee dismantle some solar panels that would then be installed on the *Moaning Lisa*, when Griffin's gravelly voice called from below.

"Need any help up there?" he asked.

"I think we're okay. We're almost done."

"Good, because I wasn't going to climb up there anyway." He smiled broadly.

"Are you afraid of *heights*?" Eliana asked.

"Not at all," he said. "It's ladders I'm afraid of."

Eliana and Zaynab both laughed.

"It's almost dinner time," he said. "Or at least I'm hoping it is."

Several minutes later, the three of them made their way to campus. Eliana listened as Zee and Griffin talked about inverters, PV cells, and BOS. She hoped Zee wouldn't ask about the council meeting Griffin had been at.

They stopped by Knight Hall to get Captain, where she had stayed with Farah and her son, then continued on to Sloan, where, sure enough, the first people were gathering at the serving table.

Everyone was talking about the evacuation. The proposed process had been announced and posted directly after the meeting this morning.

"It's so no one person gets blamed for who is chosen and who isn't." Eliana heard someone say.

The council had decided that seven community members would each choose fourteen names from a closed box. Those community members would be chosen discreetly just before the drawing tomorrow morning.

As they walked through the dining room, Eliana savored the sight of their community members talking, laughing, and helping one another on the eve of the lottery that would take most of them away. How different things would be this time tomorrow.

It happened as Griffin and Eliana were on flotsam duty, picking up debris that floated up to the surface and washed upon the embankments. She always felt it in the pit of her stomach first: a sense of unease, imbalance.

"Did you feel that?" she asked Griffin.

He stopped for a moment. "I feel it."

The water sloshed a little harder against the boats, and Captain barked at the air with her tail tucked under. Others around them noticed the odd sensation, too; she heard the murmurings of concern. The tremors were far away enough that one could almost miss them. And sometimes they did, and the later waves slapped them in surprise.

"We'd better head inland. You never know," Eliana said. Usually, the waves took some time to travel across the waters, hit their walls, and rush up the floodplain. But there was no way to know where the tremor had originated, so no way to know when the waves would reach them.

They gathered up what they could easily carry and made their way back to the campus.

Everyone staying in Sloan seemed to be gathered outside the dimly lit halls, speculating and worrying. It always seemed like the same few were responsible for keeping everyone else calm. Eliana was one of those people despite the fact that she was the most terrified of all.

There was nothing more to do but wait and see.

Griffin nudged Eliana awake. "Quietly," he whispered.

Eliana rolled off the sofa where they had slept entwined and followed him. They crept down the hallway, careful not to wake sleeping families, and went up the stairs to the roof.

The air smelled of petrol, rotten eggs, and an astringent chemical smell that left a metallic taste in her mouth. Keith was already up there, his walkie buzzing with the voices of the other watchers. They stood near the roof's edge, Griffin several feet from the edge, and looked out at the darkness.

It seemed even the moon had hunkered down safe from this night because it held no light for them to see by. They could only hear as the water slammed against the land and splashed over the wall. Creaking and cracking, scraping and screeching, of structures giving way, or of once-submerged debris fighting its way back to land.

Suddenly, Mira burst through the door to the roof. She swept the rooftop with her flashlight."She's gone!"

"What? Who?" Eliana's mind raced. Rania? Zee? Or maybe she meant Captain, who was staying with the girls that night.

"Zee! She's gone. Captain too, I think—I don't know, I didn't see her. The door was open. I thought she might have come up here." Mira's voice was panic-stricken.

They all ran downstairs and poured out the main doors. The air was strangely still against the sounds that assailed them. Several other people appeared with flashlights, all shouting for Zee.

Eliana's heart was in her throat and threatening to choke her.

Griffin appeared beside her. He grasped her wrist and stayed tight to her. "We'll find them," he said.

Flashlight beams bounced in all directions, and the turbulence of light, sound, smell, and dread eddied through Eliana. This time, though, she had an anchor, and it wasn't on her chest. She received Griffin's assurance, shared his fear, and carried on with strength.

And then they saw beams of light pointing at them.

"Zee??" Mira screamed.

"Amma! I'm here!"

All flashlight beams shone on her and the dog in her arms.

"What the hell were you doing?" Mira shouted.

"I was coming up to the roof. I wanted to see. I thought Captain would stay with Rania, but she didn't. She bolted out the door, and somehow she got out. I don't know, a door was open, I guess," Zaynab said in a whoosh. "I couldn't let her be out there on her own; she's just a little thing." She broke into copious tears, her fright coming to a head now that she was safe. She handed Captain over to Griffin.

He took the dog and leaned down to kiss Zaynab on the forehead. "You're my hero," he said.

Eliana hugged them both together, Mira joining in, and when Rania ducked under her mother's arm, Eliana felt the broken pieces in her clicking back together.

The sun had not yet begun to peek over the horizon when Eliana finally slithered out of bed and quickly got dressed. She wasn't sure she had slept at all between the harrowing events last night, and the disorienting emotions tangling and twisting through her like restless currents pulling her in every direction.

She had already had inklings of apprehension about her decision since that first morning waking up beside Griffin. However, she knew what she faced on this spit of land. Out there was an abyss where any number of things could happen. Yet, she couldn't deny her longing for Griffin, a new life where she couldn't hear the water lapping at the shores. She hadn't felt hope for a long time, and that hope came from what she saw in Griffin, Mira, and her girls.

She walked to the seawall, where water sloshed from underneath. Mud bubbled up when she tamped her foot down. Uprooted trees, vinyl siding, and vegetation littered the embankment, along with household trash, like bottles and egg cartons. She followed the wall until she reached the swampy cemetery, by which time she could turn off her flashlight and walk in the light of the rising sun, fear and hope battling it out inside her.

As she reached the center of campus, she saw Minho. He waved to her, swinging his whole arm back and forth.

"Come on, we'll be the first in line!" he said. Minho's wife and six-year-old son had had the opportunity to leave four months earlier, and Minho had waited patiently, but despairingly for this next opportunity. Eliana left her own deliberation unspoken and followed him through the door.

Joyce, Keith, and Aidan sat at a long table waiting, and sure enough, Minho was the first. Eliana watched as he wrote his name on a slip of paper, put it to his forehead, and dropped it in the box.

How could she put her name in? There were people who desperately wanted to leave. They had been waiting while she was still deciding what she wanted, what she could brave.

Griffin emerged from the student aid office and sat down beside Keith. He handed a slip of paper to Scarlett, the five-year-old daughter of a homesteader who had put her own name in the lottery she had previously said she would not participate in. Griffin held the slip of paper down as the little girl concentrated so hard to write her name. And though knowing such a young child would automatically be chosen if the parent was, he held the box down to her height so she could drop it in.

That's when Eliana decided. Her stomach roiled like a cauldron, but she walked over to the table and wrote her name. Griffin held the box for her, much as he had for Scarlett. He touched her hand as she put it in and looked into her eyes. "I'm glad you came," he said.

The atrium of the student center was filled with the colony's community members. If ever the colony felt crowded, it was now; nervous laughter and small talk floated around, excited conversations ricocheted. Some people had their two bags of possessions with them. Even some of the homesteaders had come out for the social occasion.

One hundred ninety-eight people desperate to leave, and room among six boats to cram only one hundred and fifty-four. Eliana feared the anger and violence that might ensue, no matter the equitable way they decided to do this. More boats would surely come, but would they come in time?

Griffin stood with Joyce in front of the gallery of windows that let in the diffused afternoon light of the September morning, and a small crowd of people, whom Eliana assumed were those who volunteered to draw names, stood at the ready. Joyce had a wide smile pasted on her face, which meant she must be nervous about the process and its outcome, too.

Mira and the girls arrived and stood with Eliana. Mira pulled her into a fierce hug. Just then, Keith entered carrying the simple lockbox, and the crowd grew quieter.

"Hey folks, are we ready?" he said.

Joyce stepped up beside Keith and said, "I first want to say to everyone," she cleared her throat, "that we have to remember who we are as people, as a community. Let's remain true to that no matter what happens here this morning. And remember that if your name is not called, these boats will be turning right back around." She smiled at the crowd, looked at her feet, and stepped back next to Griffin.

There was a smattering of applause, and Keith cleared his throat. He beckoned for Darrien to come closer, and then he opened the lid of the box. Darrien chose five slips of paper at once and read them out in a loud, clear voice.

Anita Tannen read next. She chose a name and read it aloud before choosing the next. As names were called, some people clapped, some let out a whoop, and, in the background, there was a low volume of chatter. Jan Redman, Glen Huang, and Lynsie Bolt read off their five names.

"Rania Amin," Wren Anderson called out during her pick.

Mira hugged Rania and put an arm around her.

"Joyce Carmine," another read.

There were still many to choose from, but Eliana noticed the volume had died down between names. There was no longer the chatter or good cheers. People were getting anxious. Even she felt her name might not get chosen, after all her deliberation and self-doubt. And it would only be right; she didn't deserve to go after changing her mind.

She knew she wouldn't hear Griffin's name; he was the pilot of a boat, so he was a given. She thought about Minho and said a silent wish for his name to be called.

"Mira Amin."

Rania let out a little cry and she and Zaynab both hugged their mom.

"Minho Kim," Laurie Crestler called.

Eliana was now sure she would get called. Between Minho, Joyce, and Mira, and the girls, she knew it would somehow work out, as if Minho were the lucky charm.

Many more names were called, and still, Eliana did not hear hers. Mira looked over at her in concern, but Eliana felt sure her name would be called at any moment.

"Thandie Bolton."

"Jason Lam."

And then she heard it; "Eliana Prewett."

Another name was called, and another, but she did not hear because she felt at once elated and sick to her stomach with dread. Mira grabbed her hand and squeezed it, holding it tight. People were pushing them forward toward Keith and his little steel lockbox. There were shouts and cries and wailing. Eliana was barely aware of it, though; her vision seemed to be closing in on itself, and her head felt like it would float off.

And then she heard Mira cry out. She turned and saw Mira crumple. Eliana caught her and put her back on her feet. Rania and Zaynab took their mom in their arms. It was then Eliana realized that she had not heard Zaynab's name called.

Amidst other shouts and cries, Eliana's focus sharpened. Griffin waved from across the room.

Zaynab was comforting her mother. "As soon as they drop you all off, they'll turn the boats right back around for the rest of us. It's going to be okay." She sounded like she was also trying to convince herself.

"We'll all just stay," Rania said. "We're not going without you."

A woman shouted and began cursing at someone, probably anyone she could blame for her outcome.

"No. We'll get you on. What's one more person? You'll hardly take any room. They'll understand," Mira said manically.

Zaynab shook her head. "Amma, no. Then everyone will expect the same treatment. We're not doing that."

"Then we'll sneak you on," Mira hissed.

"No," Eliana said. "Zaynab, you'll go in my place."

What was she doing? This was her chance at a sort of happiness she had thought was impossible.

"No!" Zaynab shouted, clutching Eliana's arms.

Eliana saw Griffin weaving his way towards her.

"No," Mira said. "You take the girls."

Eliana shook her head. Rania hugged her mom tighter.

"I trust you like a sister. You will take care of them and keep them safe until I get there."

Griffin had awakened emotions in Eliana that she thought were dead. He had opened up new possibilities for her. Because of him, she had chosen to face her fear. But she could not possibly allow Zaynab to stay here without her family.

"Listen. I didn't even want to go, remember? When I heard my name just now, I panicked. Imagine what will happen once I get out in the middle of the water!"

"See mom? She's right," Rania said.

"Zaynab is taking my spot." Eliana's words caught in her throat. "If I feel ready, I will get on the next boat." Tears stung her eyes.

Rania released her mom and smooshed herself against Eliana. "Thank you," she said.

Eliana hugged the girl tight. "Tell Joyce," she whispered into the girl's hair. She pulled herself away, then rushed toward the exit before Griffin could reach her and before she could change her mind.

Eliana took the stairs slowly, no longer in any rush. It would be like the last few weeks had never happened. She had always been good at compartmentalizing life; she was good at keeping busy.

Blinded by tears, she did not want to cry, Eliana ran. Staying was the right thing, the only thing she could do. Griffin was a dream; Mira and the girls were family. A fling, that's all it was—a fond memory to hold onto.

She ran up the metal stairway to the top of the church.

Under the cross, she watched people swarm to the boats and then board. The *Saviour Complex*'s appointed crew adjusted tarps and pulled rigging. A blooming sob filled her chest, but she bottled it up and blew it out through her mouth.

She would just keep busy. Now that so many had left, there were fewer people to do what needed to be done to keep things running. Roles were now unfilled. There would at once be less work and more work—plenty to keep her busy until the sadness passed. Except, she wasn't sad. She was angry.Hot tears rolled down her cheeks. A great big sob tore free, almost choking her. She couldn't watch the boats go. She radiated her well wishes for a safe journey, but she saved herself from that last pain. A faint whimper sounded. It hadn't come from Eliana. It came from below her. Eliana paused to listen. There it was again. And then she heard the distinctive whine of a dog. Eliana rose to her knees and scurried to the catwalk. Had Captain gotten spooked and bolted off? Eliana leaned over the walkway. Captain stood below, her tail wagging. She jumped and circled, unable to get up on her own. "Oh my God!" Eliana scrambled on her hands and knees. "Wait! Captain, stay!" Eliana hurried for the stairs. It was too late. The boats were surely out on the water. Eliana threw the door open. "Captain!" she yelled...right into Griffin's face. He ducked like she'd thrown a punch. "Whoa," he said. "She's right here." "Wh... Why are you here?" Eliana stammered. "I just couldn't stand the thought..." He dropped a stack of canvas next to the door and pulled a hammer from his belt. "...of you up here in your lighthouse without curtains."

# YOU KNOW, HYPOTHETICALLY SPEAKING

## By R.C. Calvio

WHEN I MEET WITH the Earth goddess, I don't hold any pretense over my control of the matter. She comes to me in my sleep, no more gentle about it than a beast that hunts you down, mauls you, and then leaves you for dead. There is no taming or controlling her. Like the other gods in our family, she will do what she wants. When you have committed a sin against her as grave as I have, then you know this fact intimately well. If you haven't, it goes a bit like this...

You become restless, never settled in one place. Sweat beads at your back when you watch the sun go down. Any thought of hunger is erased because your stomach is churning so badly you might just throw up. The sun lowers behind the trees or the houses or the mountains, wherever you happen to be, and you know: it's hunting time.

And you are woefully unprepared, even though you promised

yourself this morning that tonight would be different. It won't be. It never is. That doesn't stop the hope that maybe this time your prayers to the other gods will protect you. Except they know you've never been one to pray, that the only god you've ever worshiped was yourself, and if you can't save yourself, there is nothing they can do. They turn a blind eye. There is no hiding from Earth, no matter that you were once fearsome and her equal. You are nothing now.

You are terrified. Your eyes close because even though you *know* she waits for you, your body remembers the comfort she once gave you. It remembers her arms around you when she sang you to sleep, her steady presence when you took your first steps. These are the memories that give her an opening to hold you captive.

You stand in a forest so old and thick there is no telling where you are in relation to the rest of the world. There is certainly no sight of the sun or sky. Yet there you are, amid gnarled branches and roots that curl and dig into the dirt. You hear the whisper of your breath and the pounding of your pulse, and the woods can hear it, too. The stagnant air is so ancient there is no telling who breathed it first, but surely it was sweeter then. Now, it's like gasping for a desperate breath beneath water.

Your instincts scream for you to flee, and it is only when your eyes adjust that you realize Death once roamed this place. His presence lingers: tree skeletons left to decay against their growing cousins, a boulder that is twice your size split into two clean halves, and a jagged scar in the ground, wide enough for two horses to walk abreast. When you peer into it, it's bottomless, and there is no way you are anywhere close to a place on Earth, but somewhere alien and unwelcoming.

Except the sinister bit is that you know this place. You know it well, and yet you hesitate to call it home. How could you? You renounced that right when you took Death's blessing and made the very crevasse you stare into. You hope you are sure-footed enough to walk along its edge. Following it is the fastest way out. The risk is worth avoiding the memories.

There was a time when you played between these roots as a child and the forest ate up your laughter. You didn't notice because you were too busy making ships and trains and castles out of the trees and rocks. You created your enemies and you always won, and you never considered that one day this place would fight against you, that one day it would *hate* you. That now every step deeper into its heart, you poison it and it poisons you in return; a back and forth of entities that have survived the insurmountable. Only one of you was malicious about it, and it wasn't the forest, because nature could be harsh and cold but it couldn't be evil.

The goddess knows this is the last place you want to be, which is why she's put you here. There is no comfort in the memories of growing and laughing here, of training for your place among the gods. You forfeited all comfort the moment a thrill walked down your spine when you realized how fragile it all was. You were banished from here when Death took notice.

You keep moving. It's easier to push onward and fake the ease with which you used to make this place yours. It's easier to hop and skip over roots without looking down, ignoring the forest's attempts to trip you, to drag you into the crevasse where you belong. It's easier to look up at the canopy instead and maybe whisper an apology, or maybe not, and let that "maybe" be enough. To apologize in earnest would be admitting the truth of your feelings, and there is no way you can unbox that in this place that would love to tear you apart.

The forest is seeking your confession. A presence, an energy, brushes at the back of your neck, at your ear, and then pokes insistently at the corner of your mouth. Your lips are the part of your body that always betrays your thoughts, always ghost upwards at your first falsehood. They can't hide your secrets even when you lie to yourself over and over that you are not upset, that you have no reason to cry, and that worse things have happened to you. It's a tic that is barely noticeable to the ones who love you, but the forest sees all and it has no patience for your lies.

The forest pokes and pokes until you bite your lip to make it stop twitching. You swallow down the lump of anger, and push yourself off a root like a springboard over your thoughts. You just want to get out of here. If you were to confess anything, it would be in the safety of your room, and never would you utter it. You would lock it between pages of a sketchbook where you keep your secrets. It's safest there.

The forest narrows around you, trying to squeeze the truth out of you or push you over the edge, whichever comes first. You press your lips shut and stomp on rocks and wayward twigs towards the only source of light. On the other side is home. You know this in your soul. The light calls to you and so you run to it. You run fast and ignore your lungs that want to burst, and your ankles that twinge whenever your feet land on rocks at odd angles. None of it matters because just on the other side is safety and warmth and comfort.

You burst through with a smile on your face, triumphant that you beat your fear of a place that never had dominion over you. As you breathe in open air, you wonder why you were ever concerned in the first place. Trees can't hurt you. You were practically born beneath their branches. You learned life's hardest lessons there. You turn back, prepared to make some kind of smart remark. Bravado is your best shield, and the mere idea of using it calms your racing heart before you've opened your mouth to speak.

That is when you notice the roots wrapped tight around your legs, digging into your skin and drinking the red, *red* blood that trickles towards your foot. These same roots are around your arms, your ribs, your neck. When you face forward to the place where safety lay, there is the goddess staring at you with eyes brighter than your own.

She looks familiar. She has hair like you, long and braided, and skin like you even if it is a shade browner. She wears her anger and disappointment like a second and third skin, consumed so wholly by her emotions that she can't split her time between them. She is upset with you and you know why, but neither of you says anything. You can feel your lump of rage scrabble its way back up your throat, indigestible.

Because you know what? You feel like shit. To the point where it has become part of your personality instead of being a passing mood. It has warped you deep inside, in places that you can and cannot see, and knowing this is devastating because you used to *love* yourself and *know* yourself, and now neither of those things are true. You can't stand yourself and you don't trust yourself, and you know that you will never be able to again.

You are so *angry* at this goddess who has the *nerve* to be disappointed in you, angry at you, and believe her feelings are the most important feelings you will ever have to address. When the reality is what she feels towards you could never hold a candle to what you feel towards yourself.

She is standing there feeling righteous and important while she is surrounded by wolves that are looking at you with hunger. Their eyes are vacant, like they never knew you to be one of them, when you know they were there for your first steps, guarding you while the gods taught you everything you needed to know to make them proud.

She thinks Death stole you away, nurtured your innate selfishness and taught you to be fearless. She forgets that the qualities she instilled to make you a powerful god, are the same qualities that drove you to search for more, and that it was only natural for you to look to her brother. The world is ugly and bitter and complicated, and it is both about and not about you, because you hold the unique ability to just *make* things happen; and it was fun until it wasn't because now you know the faces and names of every person who has been hurt simply for existing in the path of your hubris.

She shoves the cruel parts of yourself in your face, demanding an explanation she has never been owed. You want to yell at her, to rip her to pieces the same way she is doing to you despite not lifting a finger.

She tells you that you need to be punished; as if this is the first time you have ever considered the idea. Of course, you need to be punished. You sinned. You did something evil because something evil looked inside you and saw that it was only natural. Yet what you also understand is she has no right to punish you because she and a family of Others created you to be this way. She could have stepped in at any point, could have just as easily taken you from Death and nurtured your innate kindness.

The injustice of it all builds in you until your skin heats and the corner of your mouth makes you smile at the hypocrisy of it all. She is going to use the wolves against you. You know to look for vengeance in the glint of her eye and the hardness of her mouth and the power of her stance and the puff of her chest. That look is all too familiar because you used to see it in the mirror. Its familiarity rots in your soul and body, so when you see the blood trickling down your legs turn black, you are not surprised.

She tells you this is for the good of everyone you hurt. She tells you that wolves take care of problems within the pack, that it is only natural. When the beasts launch themselves and sink their teeth into you, she tells you that you will be stripped of all that built you—your power, your ambition, and your passion for a world that has always been scared of you—tools you've only just begun to learn to wield gently and for others. There will be nothing left, and she says this is the kindest punishment. Yet what she will never understand is she is merely ripping away the last vestiges of who you used to be; the last parts of yourself that you loved.

You are *angry*, but you cannot fight back. You are essentially this lifeless *thing*, now. You know her rage comes from a place of fear and pain. You know it intimately, especially now that it is all that she has left for you. These feelings are "you" now, and you know it is wrong, but she doesn't. She thinks it is "kind."

She leaves you mauled and bleeding. The roots recede from your body and leave your black blood behind. The forest no longer wants anything to do with you. It cannot recognize you. You are unnatural.

…Then you wake up.

The sky is bright and your love is asleep beside you, embodying forgiveness and all that is beautiful in the world. You sit up and yawn and stretch and shuffle down to the kitchen after sneaking the softest kiss to their mouth. You start up the coffee pot and read the reports for the day, and you let it all disappear from your mind. You've been hunted and mauled and left for dead, but you are awake and have another day to get through.

Despite your wishful thinking, you know even the daylight won't protect you. The scars in your mind might be well hidden, but not the ones on your arms, your legs, your throat, where claws left serrated edges and teeth left your skin pitted into hundreds of crescent moons. You don't have the power to hide, the power to do anything. You have no choice but to walk around in public, skin crawling with all the eyes that follow you wherever you go. The demand for them to *stop staring* weighs heavy behind clenched teeth....

And I don't know about you, but what bothers me the most about all of this, as I watch the coffee drip into my cup at a snail's pace, is that one day my son will ask me what happens when you anger a god. He'll have figured it out the way all children discover their parents' secrets—by watching us as closely as we watch them. I won't have a good answer for him.

I'll try to lie. "I don't know, can't say I've ever done it."

He'll know I'm lying because he's my kid and he knows all my tells better than any old forest. We'll look each other in the eye. "Be serious," he'll say, because he'll still be young and won't have a concept of how scary "serious" is.

"Well..." it'll be more of a sound than a word. The memories, the nightmare, the truth, all of it will get stuck in my throat, fighting to get out. "*Hypothetically* speaking..." And in all the chaos of what I've been through every single night for the past fifteen years, what will stand out most, because it always does, is that the goddess changes her hairstyle. It doesn't always suit her face.

# HUNTING THE RIDER ON THE WHITE HORSE

## By Roxane Llanque

*But now something came toward me on the dike. I heard nothing, but ever more clearly as the light of the half-moon grew sharper, I thought I could make out a dark shape, and soon, as it came nearer, I saw it. It sat on a horse, a high-boned, haggard white horse. A dark mantle fluttered across the figure's shoulders, and as he flew past, two burning eyes stared at me out of a pale face. Who was that? What did he want? And now I suddenly realized that I had heard no hoofbeats, no panting of the horse; and yet horse and rider had galloped past me!*

**Theodor Storm, *The Rider on the White Horse***

I HALTED MY WHITE mare only when the Wadden Seaspray had soaked my woollen pants black and her bright fur grey. The North Frisian wind had long since whipped the hood off my head, and both our manes were a tangled mess. The coming storm had cleansed the beach e of humans, and even my horse regarded me critically for having steered her here, just as the

145

old man who loaned me the mare and the alewife who sold me the bottle of mulled beer had done. I knew that neither of them would understand if I told them I had wanted to see the ghost of the *Schimmelreiter* since I was a child; I knew that only a sea storm would grant me the chance to come near him.

I dismounted and gently pressed my face to the mare's muzzle to calm her. I led her to the nearest dune that would offer some semblance of protection from the elements. There, I knelt in the white sand, drank from the mulled beer, and opened my beloved book in my lap, its pages fighting the wind. I had first read *The Rider on the White Horse* as a child: the legend of the cursed genius Dikemaster who spent his life protecting the Frisian islanders by building dikes of a calibre never seen before, who tore up the old order of things and gifted a safer way of life to the people of the Wadden Sea. The dikes before him had met force by force; angry waves would clash against steep, stubborn walls, only to jump all the higher. Hauke Haien's dike, though, had met them with a gentle slope, an unassuming welcome where the waves would lose most of their power only to softly slide back and rejoin the ocean.

Of course, they hated him for it; for taking away the mighty vision of the old dikes to replace them with costly modern nonsense. And their grudge and superstitions that turned anyone going against them into a creature of the netherworld hardened his heart. In turn, he worked them hard, and the Frisians would curse him and his ghostly white horse that let only the Dikemaster near it, its fiery eyes spying everything. The fear of them was stronger than the nonrepudiation of the success and protection his grand undertaking brought them.

I startled when my mare neighed and knelt next to me in the sand, nervously nudging my shoulder. Horses rarely laid down; did she fear the storm? That I would keep her here?

I hugged her neck. Horses feel if their rider is afraid; perhaps mine sincerely worried for my defying calm.

Between the strands of her flying mane, I gazed out to the sea, waves crashing higher and higher. On the darkening horizon, it was as if someone had cut a triangle into the sky, for in its confines, I could see the first rain slicing open the dark clouds.

The legend said that the ghost of the Dikemaster would gallop over the *koog* he built whenever it was in danger of being pierced by the watery lances of the Wadden Sea. I looked over my shoulder… but the dike behind me stood empty and strong.

The truth was I had longed to see the ghost since I read of him as a child because I felt a kinship with him. I knew what it felt like to be made a living ghost for being different and questioning that which was considered normal. I don't wish to brag; I was no genius like he clearly was. Just more learned and curious than the other children deemed acceptable. I was silent and strange to them, queer in both the old and the new sense of the word. Only many years later, I would understand that the children hadn't ostracised me because they were afraid of the shy, harmless girl I'd been; they were afraid to be other and out like me . Like the Frisians had been of Hauke Haien.

Unlike him, I left.

Unlike him, I needed to in order to embrace who I was without fear, to use the gifts I was given. My journeys over the world cast loose the storm within me. The whirlwind of passions and challenges, the will to speak what no one wanted spoken. These days I knew I talked too much. Perhaps all the things the girl I used to be had desperately wanted to say still bubbled up from some deep, painful place inside me, afraid she would lose her voice again. But the storm quieted my ever-roaming thoughts.

Most people now say they are atheists, but they will always follow the pagan way of offering the outcasts up to a higher force so they may be spared. From storms, from judgement, from ostracization. The Dikemaster had refused to imprison a living thing in his new dike as tradition had demanded, which only deepened the alienation of his people. With time, he lost his strength to constantly fight for the work he knew had to be done, so finally, he gave in to them, not repairing what they deemed a minor fault in the embankment, which he knew in his heart to be dire. And in swift retaliation for his repose, a great storm of the North Sea pierced his dike where he was weak, but once.

He rode into the flood and asked God to take him and spare the others, and finally, was sacrificed to satisfy the people's endless fear.

The waves from the sea snaked higher up the beach now, one wetting my boots. My mare neighed so insistently I had to laugh and hug her. "Shhh, don't worry. I won't let the sea sweep us away."

With an untimely sunset upon us, I stood up, the full force of the wind nearly toppling me back into the dunes. I hesitated, then bowed down and gently pressed my hand into the waves coming for me. A salute and a goodbye, for I refused to be an offering to the fearful masses.

I mounted my white horse and steered her back towards the dike, her muscles looser with the tangible relief of leaving the stormy sea behind. As we galloped down the Dikemaster's *koog*, I hoped that when he saw another rider on a white horse here in the storm… he would rest knowing we were on watch.

# THE GRAY CLOAK
## By Amy Gordon

*HEAR ME NOW*: THAT time Hades brought me down into the Underworld—all that has been told or written about that journey is false.

To begin:

For many years, I, the goddess of Spring, ran barefoot in the woods and meadows. I rose early, for I never tired of watching Helios and his winged horses pull the sun up into the sky. I swam with the river nymphs and climbed trees or sat in my mother's sacred grove, listening to the dryads tell their stories.

But there came a day when I experienced a new and disconcerting sensation—one that I find difficult to explain. An invisible swath of wool had wrapped itself about me, hampering my movements. In my mind's eye, I saw it as a heavy, gray cloak. When I tried to run or swim, this invisible cloak weighed me down. It tangled me as I tried to climb trees. The more I fought against it, the more it clung, binding me with fist-like knots.

I wished I could speak of this affliction to my mother. After all, she was the goddess of growing things, and that's what I was—a growing thing. I needed her to comfort me and tell me it was customary for all gods sometimes to feel this way. Or perhaps I had been cursed, and she might know how to release me.

But my poor mother—I could not approach her. The Fates had led her to walk one afternoon in a newly-cut field of hay, and there she had met a young god. I will not go into the details of that story, for it is recounted elsewhere, but I will simply say there was a new-found lightness to her being—and that is why Zeus, my father, struck that young god through the heart with a thunderbolt. So no—now was not the time to distress my mother with a tale of a gray cloak that only I could see.

I began to sleep late in the mornings, and then later and later into the afternoons, and still I slept, even as Helios lowered the sun. By nightfall, it was only hunger that drove me from my bed.

One night, out of boredom and restlessness, I decided to explore the wooded hillside behind our house, hoping for what I scarcely knew. More accustomed to day than night, I jumped at every sound, imagining malevolent spirits behind every tree. In spite of this, I made myself return to the woods night after night, determined to grow less afraid. And before long, I was rewarded. After the sun goes down, the Earth gives up its marvelous scents. The voices of tree frogs, crickets, owls, and foxes filled my ears, each imparting important secrets of spring that I had never learned before.

But though the creatures of the night kept me good company, I was lonely for my own kind. I was, therefore, elated one evening to see my older sister, Artemis, roving through a moonlit coppice, a stag running by her side.

I followed her, though it was a challenge to keep up with her. She was wiry and fit. Even her face was lean. No one would have been tempted to pinch her cheeks the way Aunt Athena was always pinching mine when she came down from Olympus for a visit.

I was gasping by the time she finally stopped for a drink of water at a woodland pool.

As I threw myself down on the bank beside her, she said, "A bit out of shape, are we?"

"I've been lazing about, sleeping a lot," I admitted. Then screwing up my courage, I said, "Temmy, would you mind if I asked you something?"

"Don't know yet," said Artemis in her clipped and serious way.

"Did you—did you ever feel as if you were wearing a long, gray cloak?"

"A *what*?"

"Like your skin was closing in on you, or maybe you were in the wrong skin or the wrong body?"

Artemis narrowed her eyes at me. "Do you want to shape-shift? Into a boy, perhaps?"

"Oh—no—I don't think so. I mean, it would be fun for a while, but I don't think I'd want to be a boy all the time. I like being a girl. Or at least I used to like it."

Looking thoughtful, Artemis tossed a twig into the pool. The ripples turned silver, caught in the moonlight. "Now that you mention it, Perse, I do remember feeling awkward and clumsy when I was your age."

"*You* did?"

"Well, yes." Artemis lowered her bow, and her eyes seemed to fill with moonlight. "That's why I took to the woods at night. It was the only time some manly youth wasn't telling me how I could run faster if I held my arms just so or how I ought to hold my bow, even though I've always been a better shot than any of them."

Artemis laughed. "I finally discovered I could get away from all of it by coming out into the woods at night. For the first time in my life, I could concentrate on the *essence* of things—look," she said, pointing. "You see how that moonlight is shining on the water? It *fills* you. And if you get lost, you always have the Great Bear above you to guide you." She looked up, and I looked up with her. A patch of night sky caught between the tops of trees held a cluster of stars. "The moment I actually began to *see* and *feel* the world around me, Persephone, my body lightened, and I could run through the woods as gracefully as any deer."

Lowering its head, the stag beside Artemis nudged her shoulder. "But listen, Perse. I must be off as Helios will mount the sky ere long."

And with that, she leaped up and took off, as fleet as the stag she followed.

The next evening, I wandered over to my mother's sacred grove, a lovely wood with a stream that meandered along beside it.

Coming upon a great, wide stump, I sat down. Then, I heard a rustling voice coming from a small oak tree.

"Welcome, daughter of Demeter," said the dryad. "We don't usually see you by moonlight. What brings you here?"

I wanted to tell her about the gray cloak, but instead, I said, "My mother hasn't been well. I'm looking for some company."

"We could tell you some stories," said the dryad. "For instance, do you know the story of our sister who once lived in the tree where you are sitting now?"

I shook my head and told her no.

"Have you not heard of Erysikthon?" the dryad asked. Again, I shook my head.

"Let me tell you then. Erysikhthon was one of those tiresome kings who was used to getting what he wanted, and what he wanted most of all was to build a feast-hall so grand it would bring him fame and fortune. So he roamed about the countryside, searching for a tree that he could use for timbers. Alas, he found what he was looking for right here in this very grove—a giant oak that had taken centuries to grow."

I looked down at the stump with its many rings, too many for me to count.

"We dryads used to dance around it, hand in hand. It took some fifty of us to circle its girth. It towered above all the other trees. But Erysikthon swung his blade, and then again. The third time, blood spurted from its trunk, for he had struck our sister who lived within. We begged your mother to punish the man and believe me, it did not take much persuading. Demeter was as angry as we were. She set her serpents to seek out Limos, the god of Hunger. Though your mother and Limos never meet, their goals in life being very different—the one to feed, and the other to starve—she knew it always amuses Limos to see what trouble she can cause."

The dryad paused for a moment to catch her breath. All the trees in the grove and the reeds along the edge of the stream seemed to lean in closer to listen.

"Erysikthon built his feast-hall," the dryad continued. "And it was large enough to seat one hundred men. One night, Limos found him sleeping soundly in a bed made from the oak's sturdy timbers. Oh, how she wound about him, wrapping him in her arms. Perhaps he dreamed she was his true love—who knows? But from then on, no matter what he ate, he was never sated. He gorged himself on heifers and mules, a racing horse. Even a poor old cat! The more he devoured, the more he craved. And in time, he ate through all his wealth."

The dryad laughed a cold laugh that sent a shiver through me.

"Finally, in desperation, he tried to sell his own daughter—can you imagine that? But Persephone, your uncle Poseidon took pity on her and gave her the power to shift into the shape of any creature she desired. You'd think she would have used that power to escape, but she was a devoted daughter, indeed, for she chose to be a fisherman so she could feed her father fish. She then became a gull and brought him clamshells. Even so, that was not enough. Erysikhthon began to gnaw on his own arms and legs until he was nothing more than bones and skin. The wrath of

Demeter was finally appeased. She had wreaked her vengeance."

Truthfully, the story made me feel sick. The cloak snugged even more tightly against my body, and I felt as if I couldn't breathe. I got up and walked as quickly as I could away from the grove.

Rather than returning to the grove the next evening, I chose to play tag with a zephyr. The young breeze was simple and undemanding, and he made me laugh. I almost forgot about the annoyance of the cloak as I grew skilled at finding my way through the maze of trees in the dark. It was lovely, too, being surrounded by fireflies—those bright and dancing spirits. *Artemis*, I thought, *you were right*. Perhaps from now on, I would only walk about in the night. Or perhaps my father, Zeus, would shape-shift me into a firefly. Light and weightless, that is what I longed to be.

I spread my arms wide and ran in a circle, pretending I had already become so, and *bam*! I had run straight into the barrel chest of a man. I screamed, he shouted, and then he burst out laughing.

"Persephone! There you are!" the man exclaimed. "I've been looking for you everywhere."

It was so dark I couldn't make out his features, but I knew that voice. "Uncle Hades!"

He took a step toward me. "Your mother sent me to find you."

"*Really*? She actually noticed I was gone?"

"Yes, really, Persephone. She was worried."

"I'm not going home."

"No?

"It's just too depressing."

Uncle Hades cleared his throat. "Yes, well, terrible heartbreak. So sorry for your mother. Zeus is not at his best. But this works out very well for me. I've been meaning to talk to you for some time now, Persephone. I have some rather important things to tell you. So come along, down we go."

Before I could protest, Uncle Hades raised an arm, and there was a frightful groaning as the Earth opened. Then, grasping me tightly about the waist, he propelled me forward, and we stepped into nothingness.

I really don't know if it was an hour or only several minutes that we plunged down and down through darkness. It was impossible to tell, but then, there we were, standing in the Throne Room of the Palace of the Underworld, candlelight glinting off the gold pillars that supported the roof.

"Is this new?" I asked, looking down at the floor. A design of mosaic tiles had been laid down in concentric circles, each filled with fascinating-looking figures. "I don't remember seeing this the last time."

Uncle Hades nodded. "It's a representation of the Underworld inspired by a mortal named Dante. Highly imaginative, but inaccurate, of course."

It had been ages since I'd visited my uncle in the Underworld. I'd forgotten the many wonders it held. One of my favorites was a panel painted with Aunt Aphrodite seated on a bench, a dove perched on her knee, and Eros hovering near her shoulder.

And then I was taken by surprise again. For now I was staring at a girl I didn't recognize. Oh Zeus! I realized I was looking in a mirror and I was horrified.

*When did this happen? I used to be slender.*

And though I couldn't actually see the cloak in the mirror, I could feel the scratchy strands of wool straining across my breasts.

I decided right then and there never to eat again. Though Uncle Hades offered me a pomegranate, my favorite fruit, and grapes, my second favorite, I pushed them away. Oranges, figs, goat cheese—no.

"Uncle Hades, could you possibly turn me into a firefly—"

There was a sudden rumbling above our heads, and then the room began to vibrate. I clutched Uncle Hades' arm in terror.

"There, there," he said with a smile. "Don't fret. It's not Poseidon striking the Earth in a rage or anything like that. It just so happens that the Throne Room is under a highway, and it's the morning commute." Then, tugging ferociously on his black beard, he began to shout. "Cars, trucks, buses, motorcycles— those good-for-nothing mechanical mules! I have to find a place for 1.35 million shades down here every year now because of all the fatal crashes. And of course everyone who comes here thinks they're a hero and they deserve to get into Elysium."

I walked slowly across the room and sat down on Uncle Hades' throne.

"Uncle Hades—what is a 'highway'? What are 'cars and trucks?'"

"My dear child, I'm so sorry. I should have explained. On this visit I've made a point of not only traveling through layers of Earth, but also traveling through Time. Actual centuries have passed."

"*Centuries?*"

"Yes, and I can't possibly tell you how all those centuries have been filled with wars and droughts and fires and famine and floods. Not to mention drug overdoses. Diseases. Drone strikes."

Uncle Hades was pacing now around the mosaic circles on the floor.

"And don't get me started on guns. . . It's driving Charon crazy having to ferry all these souls across the Styx. He keeps begging me to hire more ferrymen, and I've tried, but no one seems to want to work anymore."

Uncle Hades' rants were famous, but I was only half listening, for I suddenly imagined that the rumbling above us was caused by a cavalcade of what Uncle Hades was calling buses, and in those buses, I pictured hundreds of young gods and goddesses going off to watch some decathlon. They were all having fun, and not one of them was weighed down like me by a gray cloak. Or coat. Or was it a jacket? My vocabulary was trying to catch up with the changing times.

"Horses," Hades was saying. "Mortals and gods alike need to go back to those great, noble beasts." He took a breath, then abruptly stopped his rant and walked over to me. "That father of yours—does he visit you often?"

"—I—"

"Ha, I knew it! He neglects you in the way he neglects all his offspring. Goes about littering the Cosmos with his DNA, and is the world better off for it? Of course not!"

"Uncle Hades. You said you had some things to tell me. And also that you brought me through Time on purpose."

Uncle Hades stared at me thoughtfully for the next few seconds and then he said, "Yes."

"Yes?"

"Let us begin. I want you to ask me a question, Persephone."

"Ask you a question?"

"Yes, that is what I said. Any question at all."

"But why?"

"Zounds, child. What is the matter with you? Asking questions is the most essential ingredient to living a meaningful life. And as an expert in Death, believe me, I know all about Life."

"Um, okay. Why do you have so many pictures of Aphrodite?"

Uncle Hades smiled, and it made him look a lot less gloomy than he usually did—almost handsome, in fact. "An excellent question," he said. "As god of the Underworld, I deal with a lot of wailing and gnashing of teeth. So what sustains me? Two Great Things. Can you guess what they are?"

"Um . . .being funny?"

Uncle Hades nodded approvingly. "Not a bad guess. There's hope for you. Humor comes in under the first Great Thing."

"What is it, Uncle Hades?"

"Eros—the fundamental, life-preserving, creative impulse. Now, you guess the second one on your own.

"Love?"

"Death."

"*Death*?"

I pummeled the base of the throne with the heels of my feet. "How can Death be more important than Love?"

"Love is a subcategory of Death—and please stop kicking my throne. Look, Persephone, all you have to do is imagine what it would be like if you lived forever. Without Death, you would never appreciate anything. *Cherish* anything. You would take everything for granted."

"But you've been alive for thousands of years, Uncle Hades. The gods don't die."

"Ah, that is a misconception, my dear."

I frowned, trying to make sense of what he was saying. "So, are you trying to tell me that Death is the most important thing in Life?"

"No, I am trying to tell you that Eros and Death are the two most sustaining things in Life, and they are inextricably mixed up with each other. But I won't stand here and try to explain anything more to you. The real reason I brought you down here is to show you the part you play in all of this."

As he finished speaking, an odd thing began to happen. Three of the paintings on the walls shimmered and then faded, and each one was replaced with a living, moving scene.

The first depicted a herd of cattle caught in snow drifts and the throne room filled with the sound of their desperate lowing.

The second showed dust swirling off a barren hillside. A child with huge eyes and a concave chest was sucking on a stone.

The third showed a sort of cathedral made of arching ribs, and gradually, I realized it was a graveyard for elephants.

"What *is* this?" I cried out. "What is happening?"

But Uncle Hades only said, "Now look in the mirror, Persephone."

Afraid, I made myself look in the mirror again. This time, instead of seeing myself, I saw my great-grandmother, Gaea. *How ancient she looked.*

And beside her stood my grandmother, Rhea. *When had she become so bent over?*

And beside her was Demeter, my mother. *Oh, Mother! Your hair! It is no longer the color of wheat—it is as gray as my coat.*

"Oh!" I cried out. "Great-grandmother is dying—and Grandmother is ill—and my mother—" For the first time I understood that my mother, too, would die one day. "Uncle Hades, the gods *do* die."

"Hush," said Uncle Hades. "You must listen to them now."

"Persephone!" They called out in unison, like the Chorus in one of our great Tragedies.

And then Gaea began to speak in her trembling, old crone's voice: "Persephone, through five stages hath the men and women of the Earth passed. The First was Gold, the second Silver. The third was Bronze. Then came the age of Heroes, followed by Iron."

"But now," chimed in Rhea, "we live in the Age of Insatiable Hungers."

"My daughter," said my mother. "The Earth is dwindling. She is being devoured. The men and women of the Earth are never sated. The more they devour, the more they crave."

Then all three said: "The Earth needs your help, Persephone, for when we die, the Earth will die, too."

My heart was pierced. As a child, I had been so carefree, skipping about, bringing Spring into the world. For centuries, that had been my role. But that was no longer enough. With both hands, I grabbed fistfuls of the fabric of the cloak, the coat, the jacket— whatever it was— clinging to me and yanked it off my shoulders.

I sat down at Uncle Hades' table and picked up a pomegranate. I imagined for a moment that in my two hands, I was holding the globe of the Earth. Then I picked up a knife and sliced it down the middle. The rows of gleaming seeds were beautiful, like the gems of the Earth.

And I thought: *There is one more great Sustaining Truth, and that is the beauty of the Earth.*

I placed one seed in my mouth, and the snow drifts in which the cows were struggling began to melt.

A second seed and green shoots sprang up on the barren hillside.

A third seed and the starving child reached for figs growing above her head and began to nourish herself.

*As I needed to nourish myself if the Earth were to become fat with life again.*

I ate, and then, jumping up from the table, I said, "Goodbye, Uncle. I am going back up into the daylight."

This, I tell you, is the true story of my journey to the Underworld. And since that time, I have worked both day and night, striving to appease the hungers of the men and women of the Earth by bringing them the great sustaining gift of Beauty.

And you, children of the Earth, after I am gone, it is up to you to carry on my work.

# THE IRIDELLE HARVESTER

## By Leslie "XPLovecat" Horn

I LACED MY BOOTS and pulled my hood over my head, tying it tightly to brace for the wind waiting for me outside.

That routine was not new; I had been doing it for the last two years. Every morning, I rushed to get ready and hiked up the mountain to the statue just before sunrise. Once the sunrise came, I was there to harvest the Iridelle root for our village.

But that day was different. That day, I did not feel like going up the mountain. I had no agency in my fate, and I did not want to get out of bed before everyone else. This role was given to me. I did not want to trek in the snow, to feel my calves burn as I made my way to the statue. Why did people have to rely on me? I did not want to see that statue's smug face as I got on my hands and knees to give thanks. I did not want to give thanks, and I did not want to dig like a desperate animal, unearthing the root from the statue's base.

And yet, I trekked.

My walking stick struck the ground with a heavy thump with

every other step I took as my feet crunched the virgin snow. The wind bit at my face, and I cursed at it.

I was too far up for the other villagers to hear me, so I let the wind know exactly what I thought about it. That it was a damn nuisance, it hurt to walk against it, and that I didn't deserve to be slapped in the face every morning by its crisp lashes.

The wind didn't stop. But I felt a little better.

When I reached the peak, the stone statue of a woman greeted me. She was only three feet tall, but a large, vibrant green aura glowed around her. The woman's smooth stone face always looked the same, but that day, I felt judgment in her eyes, like she knew I did not want to be there.

The orange and pinks of the sunrise were starting to poke out of the sky. I kneeled before the statue and ignored the woman staring into my soul as my eyes watered from the wind.

I retrieved the petite digging and extraction tools from my bag to perform my daily harvest. Bright blue petals peeked out from under the snow. I dusted them, doing my best to clear any ice. The yellow centers, their healing cores, shined, shifting to face the rising sun.

With my small trowel, I began to chip away the icy soil at the base of the flower. Frosty earth crunched and cracked, revealing softer soil underneath. Carefully loosening the soil surrounding the roots, I carved a circle around the precious flower. I gently lifted the flower, which tingled a bit as I touched it. With its roots intact, I placed it in the jar. The work was swift yet precise, always mindful of the brief window in which the root's energy was active. I had one more to go before the sun fully rose above the horizon.

Every morning I placed two jars, each holding an Iridelle root, into my bag and made the journey back down the mountain to deliver them to the village healers. That day, as I made my way back down the mountain, the direction of the wind shifted, so it was blowing against me again.

I laced my boots and yanked my hood over my head, already dreading the wind I'd soon face.

It is a blessing to be an Iridelle harvester, but that was the second day that it didn't feel like one. I had hoped my mood from the day before was a passing phase, that maybe I wouldn't have to confront my reality if apathy settled over me. But the frustration was still fully present in my body.

The village was quiet as I made my first step up the mountain. This path was well-worn from the daily treks, and its monotony weighed heavily. Air was difficult to breathe as the wind buffeted my body. And again, I paused to curse the wind. My words echoed off the side of the mountain, and cracking sounded from above. I had been trained in avoiding avalanches, and that sound was not one. The cracking was different—more like grinding stone.

I quickened my pace to reach the statue. Its once smug face was broken into pieces, a couple of blocks still floating in the wind as I approached. The wind held the pieces aloft and swaddled like a baby, rocking them slowly to the ground. I stepped back, stunned by the sheer strength of the wind, for it should not have been able to hold those pieces of stone.

Panic rose in my chest. While, yes, I was growing frustrated with my daily trek, this was not what I wanted. I did not wish for the statue to break. I grabbed at the pieces in desperation, hoping somehow, they would adhere together.

The Iridelle roots, which should have been upright at that hour, drooped lifelessly instead and were devoid of their color. I frantically looked to the sunrise. I would not make it in time. There would be no harvest today.

I slumped down next to the broken pieces of the statue. Even as I tried to hold them together on the ground, they flopped apart like they didn't want to be together anymore.

It was broken.

I was broken.

I laced my boots and wrestled with my hood, knowing the wind was out there, ready to mock me.

When I arrived with empty jars the day before, the healers were concerned. I managed to calm their worries with a lie.

"I did not make it in time. But all will be well tomorrow."

I promised something I should not have promised.

They had enough roots to care for the elders that day, but they made it clear there was no more after that.

With the rope coiled around my waist and a bottle of sticky paste I made instead of sleeping hanging from my belt, I scaled the mountain, intent on doing whatever it took to put the woman's face together.

The wind slapped me awake, and I grumbled at its cruel embrace. I reached the statue and got to work smearing paste on pieces and tying them tightly to let them dry. The statue's eyes were slightly askew, and everything about it felt and looked off. I adjusted the pieces and tried to hold them tight, only to be pushed back by a strong gust of wind. I slipped and fumbled to get my footing. When I looked back, the statue was in pieces again.

As the sun began to rise. I chanted my thanks, hoping it might work anyway.

It did not.

I laced my boots and ripped my hood over my head, cursing the wind I could already hear howling beyond my walls.

The healers were angry when I came down the mountain again with two empty jars the day before.

"Do not worry. I simply did not make it in time. I will have Iridelle tomorrow."

I should not have promised that. They did not have any Iridelle left, which meant the elders would start to degrade, and their glowing skin would start to dull.

The wind was unkind in its strength. It pushed me back,

forcing me to turn sideways to make progress. I cursed the wind.

The tiny bit of hope I had left was extinguished when I saw the broken statue, pieces scattered further apart than the day before. But I still kneeled, gathering the pieces and trying my new paste. I worked in the faint glow of the sky before the sun reached the horizon, wrapping the cloth around the statue several times so the whole figure was covered. Before me was the shape of the stone woman, covered completely in white like a part of the mountain's snow.

Then, I waited for the sun to rise.

I gave my thanks to the cloth-covered statue and thought for a moment that it might work. Perhaps it was the trick of the light, but I thought I saw a glimpse of color on the ground.

But, alas, there was no color.

There was only the white snow and the wind there to haunt me.

I laced my boots and violently pulled my hood over my head, fully aware that the wind was out there, ready to knock me back the instant I stepped outside.

I glimpsed the elders the day before, and what I saw made me unwell. The healers desperately tried other concoctions and soups to maintain their spirits and hue, but nothing but Iridelle would do. The guilt panged deep inside my soul. I had not fulfilled my duty, and now the elders were dying. This was my fault.

When I returned empty-handed for the third day in a row, one healer said, "I know you are hiding something. I can see it in your eyes."

I told her that I did not know what she meant and that she would have the root tomorrow. As I turned to leave, she grabbed my arm.

"Have you angered someone? Someone besides me, that is."

I said I had not.

But as I made my way up the mountain that morning and turned to curse at the wind, I realized maybe I hadn't angered someone—but something. I kept my mouth shut this time. I continued up the mountain and sat before the cloth-covered statue. I slowly uncovered it, hoping the paste had somehow set overnight.

It had not.

The pieces tumbled apart, and the wind whipped, pushing me down on my side.

"Have I angered you, wind?" I whispered, afraid I might hear something back.

The wind gently caressed my face, like the touch of a lover, and lowered my hood.

No. I had not angered the wind.

I had angered myself.

I grabbed a couple of pieces of the statue in my hands and cradled them to my body.

And I wept.

I cried as the sunrise came and went.

I had not been ready for the burden of the Iridelle harvester. This role, this sacrifice, was thrust upon me without my consent.

The anger had built day after day, trek after trek until I did not want the burden anymore.

Then I thought of the elders. As harvester, I was a gift to them and the village. I gazed out, absorbing the colors of the morning sky and the beauty of the mountainside.

Perhaps something can be both a burden and a blessing.

I released the statue pieces to the ground and felt a gust of wind shove into my back. The wind whooshed past my ears, picking up the statue pieces from the ground and creating a vortex of wind and statue. I was in my own pocket on the mountain as I grabbed the pieces from the wind and put the statue back together again.

It stayed in one piece, though the cracks were still visible. And soon, the Iridelle flushed with color again.

I laced my boots and let my hood hang loose, knowing the wind would help me today.

The elders were close to dying, but I promised the healers they would have their Iridelle. This time, I knew I would keep my promise.

I started my trek up the mountain and occasionally felt a nudge from the wind, making it easier to get to the statue. I enjoyed the chill and the colors in the sky. I got out my tools and said my thanks.

Then, I harvested the Iridelle, putting one in each jar.

I would have many more treks. But now I knew the blessing that I had been given.

I gave the Iridelle to the healers that day and watched as the color in the elders' skin came back brighter and bolder than before. The trek is my burden, but the harvest is my blessing.

# SPANISH MYSTIC
## By A.R. McHugh

VIVES STOOD AT THE cell window trying to discern from the quality of blackness outside how long it would be before the storm broke.

He couldn't sleep. Pressure from the coming storm—definitely rain, he thought, probably thunder and maybe some lightning— was building in his skull, under his ears, between his eyes, in his sinuses.

In the lower bunk, Mixy snored like a bus and turned over. In his twitching hand, he clutched Vives' prayer beads like a comfort blanket. Sometimes he held them and talked frantic, gentle nonsense, clicking them through his fingers as God spoke through his schizophrenia. One of the two imams thought Mixy was blessed. The other thought his MAOIs needed tweaking.

Mixy's mother and younger brother, Jelani, took it in turns to visit. When Vives was put in with Mixy Jelani asked to see him.

'Mixy said you just became a Muslim,' he said neutrally.

Vives shrugged. 'You get better food at Ramadan. More time

out of your cell.'

'You ain't gonna radicalize him, right? Cos I ain't having that. He'll be out in a couple a months and we jus' wan' im home.'

'I ain't gonna radicalize him. I ain't much of a Muslim anyway.' This was true. He couldn't follow the point of the Quran, which seemed like one long, repetitive nag session with no stories. At least the Bible had stories. Since receiving it from the visiting imam, Brother Ashraf, Vives' copy had been used as an elbow rest on the window ledge.

He felt another lurch inside his skull. There was a rainy crackle outside and the bottom of his eye sockets twinged painfully in response. At least, he thought, he was inside, warm, fed, and had company of a kind. If he'd been outside, he'd have been trying to work out where he could doss inside.

There was a rumble of thunder somewhere over White City. Mixy whimpered and buried his face in the pillow. Vives wondered who would replace him in the bottom bunk when Mixy went home to his mum and Jelani.

He put a hand against the dark window and tried to feel the world outside the Scrubs. It felt no different from the overheated buzz of male sweat and anger inside. What made the outside seem different was the idea that someone was wishing you were out there with them. Without that, everywhere was the same. It was all freedom, or all prison.

Alone on the earth, no one knew that he existed. The thought of him, Juan Luis Vives—Brother Tariq as of three weeks ago—a skinny long-haired beggar from La Cañada Real in Madrid, held no corner in even one mind, awake or asleep, anywhere. If he winked out now like a cheap torch, not a single thing would change. The only effect he'd had on earth had been bad and small, until a tourist had hung on to the wallet he'd been pickpocketing outside Selfridges and fallen under a taxi in Oxford Street. Now Vives stood at a window in a British prison, a manslaughterer, waiting for the rain.

He put his forehead on the window and wished he could cry. He riffled the pages of the Quran, which had absorbed some damp from the window and was rippled at the leading edge. He opened it at random: *are men whom neither commerce nor sale distracts from the remembrance of Allah and performance of prayer and giving of zakah.* Bloody useless. He couldn't remember what zakah was. All these bloody words—the bismillahs and the alhamdulillahs and the dhikrs and dhimmis and tasbihs—it was all just so much theatre, like a kids' nativity play or the Santa Semana, with flowery courtesy and extravagant promises about heaven. None of it seemed to weigh much with the Brothers, either, who routinely beat the shit out of infidel prisoners.

The air spaces inside his head hummed with the weather beyond Wormwood Scrubs. He was shit at living in the world but he continued to feel its moods, even when it had put him to one side. He had always felt like a string to the world's tuning fork, twisting and contracting as the atmosphere changed. No one he knew seemed to share his experience and he kept to himself the headaches, slumps and, occasionally, throat-tightening joy that came from being the smallest peg on the instrument of the weather. It seemed ridiculous to go through life fighting, intimidating, carrying out the business of being a human, and a poor one, while being so sensitive that a coming storm could drive him to this pitch.

He considered what would likely be the state of Mixy in the morning if he woke up and found that Vives had hanged himself.

If *someone* knew that I felt this, he thought, then they would know that I existed. Even if they regarded his despair as deserved, that was still better than being unknown to anything more than a Home Office database.

Why was it even important to him to be known? Most of the other prisoners had family, mates, clients, victims who knew them. It brought them little joy and the occasional beating. But there was nothing else, he thought. He was a human and that involved needs—food, shelter, comfort, recognition. It was part of one's being, not a weakness to be got over.

There were eight billion souls on Earth, he thought, and they all wanted to be known. It was impossible. Eight billion wanting to be loved, understood, to be the object of someone's happiness, someone's triumph. You only had to look at the internet to see the scale of it; something like a billion sites all saying *I want to be recognized.*

It was enough to make you turn religious. If you could just surmount the skepticism that some gigantic eye, some huge brain, was interested in *you* as you shivered in a sleeping bag in a concrete doorway, and knew you as more than the grubby hand hoping for spare change, it might be enough.

When he had been learning English in one of the prison's intermittent programs, he had read a sentence that said people were all stardust. The teacher, a well-meaning young man who lasted three weeks, had explained that it meant elements, the things everything else was made of. Vives had not understood. The dictionary hadn't helped: *polvo de estrellas* sounded like the glitter that was always on the pavement outside cheap clothes shops. Eventually he grasped that it was a fancy way of saying that there was no difference between him and a rock. We all became something else eventually.

A rock, though, had no ache to be known. Even if, eventually, he became grass growing on a government grave, or soil in the wind, then compacted to a stone, he had to endure this way of living now, this life as a man, this set of terrible needs.

He put his hand on the book again. Did Muslims play that game of opening it at random and willing it to speak? That was gambling, and Muslims didn't gamble. So he was doing a— harem? halal? hadith?—act with the book.

He wanted to cry and couldn't. He looked at the rippled book and thought, *Talk to me. Just talk.* Prisoners never say please because they know that requests are, by nature, denied. Since it was unlikely that he would ever have a visitor during his sentence, it didn't seem much to hope a book would talk to him.

Hope was a human thing. Nature didn't do hope because no part of it was subordinate to the rest. It all just was. It also didn't know itself the way humans did, he thought. The wind didn't have an idea of what it could have been if only its needs were met. It just blew.

There were the imams, of course, and the prison psychologist—if you wanted to wait two years for a thirty-minute appointment. But you didn't talk to them. You talked at them and in the intervals they produced a randomized piece of advice about observing or accepting. You could be anyone.

The clouds, the storm, the darkness, the book in his hand—if nothing in the world of people acknowledged him, he could only try objects. He opened the book.

*Or like darknesses within an unfathomable sea which is covered by waves, upon which are waves, over which are clouds—darknesses, some of them upon others. When one puts out his hand [therein], he can hardly see it. And he to whom Allah has not granted light—for him there is no light.*

It was enough. Even if it wasn't about him in the first instance, it was enough that he had asked—a tiny voice in the whole universe—and something had seemed to reflect his situation.

Something had said, 'There you are,' and mirrored where he was, like two drivers giving each other the thumbs-up in traffic.

He did not want to question it. If this seeing thing was external to him, then it was something in which he could have faith. He knew that it was unlikely to be a good thing, or a kind one, or interested in Vives' own moral qualities, but nonetheless, it was there, this impersonal eye before which he could perform his little life. It knew he was there the way a bus driver knows he has one last passenger at the end of his shift.

The sense of oversight gave him a desire to act well towards someone, since they were both objects in the eyeline of this great warder.

Acting well for someone else, he thought, might satisfy this need to be known, to be seen. Perhaps this is what was meant about charity being an act of compassion on both sides. When you extended yourself for someone, you both put a hand into the darkness and hoped to have someone take it.

The storm moved west from White City and broke over the Scrubs, and Vives found he could at last cry.

# BRING ME A DREAM
## By Dermott O'Malley

EDWARD PULLED HIS OILSKIN coat over his head to stop
the ocean water from stinging his eyes as he tried to read the
lips of the sailing master. His words were lost to a cacophony of
thunder, an angry ocean roaring and the cracking of wood as the
ship tried to hold itself together beneath their feet. Another man
rushed by, clipping Edward's shoulder and knocking him down.
His hands splashed through the water and slammed to the wood
beneath, and as he started to get up, another sailor trampled over
him. A heavy boot in the square of his back forced the air from
his chest. Edward gasped for air while he scrambled to his feet,
coughing water from his lungs while he wiped it from his face.
The sailing master was gone, but another sailor grabbed him by
the shoulders, pulled him close, and shouted directly into his
eardrum words that resembled "Abandon!" and "Ship!"

Several men were unstowing the boats at the waist of the ship.
Edward joined three of them who had a jollyboat halfway out
of its rack, ripping frantically at knots with fingers that knew

exactly how to tie and untie them but would not cooperate. A frightened cabin boy tugged at the side of the small boat, so he grabbed the boy and shouted, "Oars, boy! Fetch a pair of oars!" The boy ran for oars while he and the other men hoisted the boat out of its rack.

The men began to tie it into the arms of a lowering davit when another larger man pushed his way in. Edward recognized him as one of the ship cooks, a massive man with a large gut. The cook shoved him aside, throwing off the weight of the jollyboat. It slid from the hands of the men and fell off the deck and into the water. The cook grabbed the oars held by the young cabin boy and ripped them from his hands, sending the boy reeling overboard. The boy's mouth twisted in an inaudible scream as he splashed into the dark water and disappeared.

The cook bundled his jacket, intending to jump into the jollyboat. Edward and the other men tried to restrain him from further rash actions, but the cook resisted. He thrashed about, slamming one sailor into a railing, tumbling another to the boards, and flinging Edward to the edge of the ship. He managed to grab onto the rail as his legs flailed below him, dangling over the water. The ship heaved now in the opposite direction, so greatly that the side of the ship Edward clung to may have been closer to upright than the deck itself, but then the ship slammed back down to the ocean, the force sending shockwaves through Edward's arms. He lost his grip and prepared to join the boy in certain doom, but a flash of lightning revealed to him the grain in the jollyboat's wood, inches from his face. The world went black.

Edward dreamed of a small port town named Tunwood Landing. Frequented by the routes of merchant vessels he often sailed aboard, Edward had grown fond of it. It had a small but strong fishing community that Edward always imagined he would join one day, but the pay kept him coming back to the sea again and again. He was a carpenter, which, paired with the skills of a sailor, was a valuable trade on larger ships.

When he opened his eyes, he thought he was waking up at the town inn, but the slapping of water against the boat dragged him further from the dream. It was daytime now, and he was alone in the small boat. He tried to push himself up but a shooting pain in his right arm halted him. He clenched his teeth as he used his left to push himself to a sitting position. His right forearm kinked in the middle—forty-five degrees past straight—and the jagged edge of white bone peeked out under a flap of torn flesh. The sun's reflection off the water blinded him from the east, but to the north, west and south, nothing but water stretching out to a perfectly straight horizon. He glanced around the inside of the boat and noted he had no oars.

Edward's focus shifted back to his arm. Being a carpenter made him, on occasion, double duty as ship surgeon. In the past he had been forced to use his woodworking tools to amputate limbs less damaged than his own. He took off his coat, then his belt, and wrapped the belt around his bicep, holding the cinch tight with his teeth. He took a few quick and shallow breaths before one long and deep, held the air in, and pulled his arm straight until he heard the ends of broken bone scraping against each other. Edward released the belt from his mouth, vomited, and fell unconscious into the boat.

He woke again to the sound of a slow knocking. When he pushed himself out of the puddle of seawater, blood, and vomit, he saw coconut trees. He scrambled to his feet and out of the boat onto a sandy shore, running a short distance before stumbling and collapsing to his knees. Ignoring the pain in his arm, he laughed and spread both arms wide as if to hug the land itself. "Land!" he cried. "Oh, blessed land, I have never seen so fair a sight! Thou art a paradise on the face of the deep!" His laugh slowly rolled into sobbing tears. He gathered himself, wiped his face with his good arm, and looked around to assess.

The beach curved away from him, but not far, to his left and right. The center was dense with trees and foliage, but through them Edward could make out a horizon of water. It was an island—a small one at that. He looked out to the ocean but saw no other masses. He tied his broken arm in a sling with his belt before struggling to his feet, and began walking along the sandy shore. He walked counter-clockwise for only a few minutes before he was already on the other side. Still, he saw no other land masses. He continued counter-clockwise the same amount of time and came back to his boat.

"Perfectly round," he said aloud. "A perfectly round, impossibly small island." In all his years sailing he had never seen such a pristine island—so small and isolated in the open ocean. Grateful as he was, his hopes sank as he stared into the shadowed green circle of land before him and felt it staring back.

His first hope was to find water. He entered the trees and leafy, plant-covered ground looking for puddles or fallen coconuts, but found nothing. Looking upward, he saw a variety of trees, mostly palms and some with clusters of coconuts nestled at the tops. They looked young and green. Edward hurled rocks and sticks at the coconut clusters with his non-dominant left arm. Most throws missed, and the few that hit did not budge the fruit at all. Edward was frustrated, but the sun was getting low so he shifted his focus. He was dehydrated, but also exhausted. His right arm throbbed and he knew the ocean breeze at night would chill his waterlogged body. He needed fire as much as water and hoped it would serve as a beacon to any other survivors or passersby.

He dragged the boat up the beach and flipped it on its side against a palm. The idea of creating a fire without flint was daunting enough even if he had the use of his right arm. His frustration grew as he scraped a stick against the center of a split log to no avail. He successfully made a small trench into the wood, and even accrued a pile of wood fibers at the bottom of the well that should have ignited, but he could not work quick enough to build the heat needed. The sun had fully set and he had only a crescent of the moon to light his failing efforts before he gave up entirely. Curled up against the boat, he covered himself in his jacket and let sleep take him.

Tunwood Landing. Something about a woman there. A muddled dream that did not stick with him the moment he opened his eyes. It was still dark and quiet, but something had woken him. His pile of sticks and kindling laid before him, and in the small well of the wood was a single flame. It was perfectly still, as if it were resting on the tip of a candle's wick. Edward scrambled closer, careful not to disturb it, and shakily worked his cold fingers to gather up leaves and kindling. The flame was so small that he was afraid to breathe as he shakily held the kindle over the flame. It slowly caught, grew larger, and he dropped the bundle onto the wood as he gathered more, eventually building a sustained fire. Basking in the heat and light, he began laughing. *"I must have built some pittance of an ember,"* he thought, and cursed himself for giving up so soon. He continued feeding the fire, and with the light it shed collected enough wood and bark to last the night.

Relieved and warm, Edward laid against the boat and stared into the flames as he tried to rest more. He was thirsty, dehydration now setting in, but there was nothing he could do until morning. Closing his eyes, Edward tried to remember his dream. He imagined the taste of the cold beer at the inn he would frequent at Tunwood Landing. There were other inns that his shipmates stayed in that were either cheaper, closer to the docks, or had better ales and better beds, but there was a woman at this inn who he preferred to serve his beverages. As he drifted back to sleep, he was startled awake by the deafening crack of a gunshot.

Adrenaline propelled Edward's legs to spring up from a near sleep. His eyes darted around, but he saw no movement. Just as his heart started to slow, another loud crack. This time his eyes locked in on its source. A coconut had fallen from the tree above, thwacking the side of the boat and reverberating through the hull. It bounced and rolled toward the first fallen coconut, settling next to it in the sand.

Edward blinked and stared at the coconuts. *"I must have knocked them loose."* Using a jagged rock, he punched a hole through the top and clumsily put his mouth over it, pouring the contents down his throat. The liquid was warm, viscous and sweet. Overwhelmed with excitement, he lost half of the contents to the sand, but the rest quenched his thirst better than any drink ever had. When the liquid was gone, he scraped the inner flesh of the fruit with his fingernails and devoured it happily. He then cradled the coconut to his chest and whispered, "Thank you, thank you." The smoke from the fire and smell of sweet coconut water on his clothes and breath was whisked up in a refreshing breeze, brushing his exposed cheek lovingly as he drifted back to sleep.

When he woke, the sun had already begun to rise. The fire was reduced to embers but still glowed at its core. Edward's arm still ached in the leather belt sling. He now had some water in him and the second coconut in reserve, but his belly ached for food other than what flesh he could scrape from the young coconut. The water's edge looked light before dropping off into the darker depths, as if a reef ringed the island, so Edward took off his shirt and trousers to wade in the water and see what lay below the surface.

The water was warm; warmer than it should be in the middle of the ocean. Thirty feet out the depth plateaued at his waist and Edward reached a sheer drop-off. It was not rocky, and there was no reef, nor seemingly anything else keeping the sand in place. He waded along the edge clockwise and only found more of the same. No coral, no fish, just sand. It was as if the island existed as a lone sandbar atop the needlepoint tip of an underwater mountain, or as if it floated freely like an independent mass of sand, both of which seemed impossible.

He returned to his campsite and rested on the edge of the boat to dry before getting dressed. He pondered how long one could live off a single coconut if he could not knock another loose. As he did, the caw of a seabird startled him. A lone albatross in the distance was gliding effortlessly through the sky toward the island. Edward scrambled to find some good throwing rocks. The bird landed atop one of the trees and stretched its impressive wings, surely sore from its long journey across countless miles of open ocean, and then tucked them in snuggly at its sides to rest. Edward crept towards the tree it had perched upon, but the bird paid him no mind. He knew he would only have one brief opportunity. Edward accounted for the distance, the angle, the weight of the rock and the accuracy of his non-dominant left hand, wound up, and hurled the rock.

The rock fell short, hitting the leaves and rustling the bird. "No, no, no!" Edward cried as he wound up a second rock. The bird extended its wings again and felt for the wind as the second rock flew far to the left of it, and it began lifting off the tree as the third barely missed its foot. "No, damn you!" he screamed. The albatross was now airborne and started to make its way across the island as Edward watched helplessly.

A strange groan came from the island and the trees started creaking and swaying unnaturally. Something small flew out from the thick of the island and struck the bird. The bird careened high into the sky, and at its apex, Edward saw its headless body paused in the air before crashing down before his feet. The bird's decapitated body laid in the sand and blood poured out of its neck stump as Edward stared down at it. The creaking and rumbling slowed to a stop and all was still except for the gentle ocean breeze. "Ahoy!" he called out to the island. "Show yourself and be known!"

No response.

Edward's gaze was fixed on the heart of the island. It seemed more alive to him than before, and he felt less alone. Terrified and confused, but oddly, less alone. He slowly picked up the dead bird and studied it. A clean cut. He again stared into the forest with the bird's body dripping blood down his arm. "Th—thank you," he said carefully. Then he nodded, cleared his throat, and said again more confidently. "Yes. Thank you."

He roasted the bird and ate it ravenously. He even decided to crack open his second coconut to wash down the meat. As he finished drinking from it, a third fell into the sand behind him. "Thank you kindly," he said to the island with a smile. Two more days of this went on. Whenever he grew thirsty, a coconut would fall from a tree. When Edward got hungry again, a turtle was thrown from the water and landed upside down next to the campsite. Edward killed the turtle, drank its blood, and roasted it in the shell.

Edward tried talking to the island a few times but felt silly. "No, I'm not mad," he said to himself one night as he stared into his fire. "But the moment I speak to ye and ye start talking back I'll know it to be true!" he said with a hearty laugh, but then grew quiet as he stared cautiously into the trees, half expecting a response.

On the fourth day, Edward spotted a dot on the sea as he strolled around the beach. Shielding his eyes from the sun and squinting he became sure the shape on the horizon was that of a ship. Frantically, he gathered all the brush he could, green and dry, and built up the fire. The figure grew larger. It was traveling east initially, but as his smoke billowed it seemed to stop. The side profile of distant sails became wide as it turned towards the island. He shouted and jumped up and down. "I am saved!" he cried. "Oh, praise be, thank you, thank you, I am saved at last!"

A moan rose from the heart of the island as the ground rumbled beneath his feet. Just as he turned to look, a wave of sand rose and rushed across the beach and towered over the fire before crashing over it. The flame was extinguished and the firewood buried. He dug at the sand where his fire had been, but there was no evidence of it—no firewood, coal or ash mixed in, just sand. He ran back to the campsite and grabbed the stern of the boat, intending to drag it to the water, but it did not budge. The other end of the boat was buried in the sand, and as he pulled on it, it pulled back. It sank into the ground until Edward was yanking at the only corner remaining above the sand. Edward dug his heels in and pulled, but the boat kept sinking and his grip gave, sending him reeling back. He landed on his backside as the sand finished swallowing the ship.

"Damn you!" He turned towards the ship on the horizon for only a moment before making a dash for the water. He heard a noise coming from the trees behind him but did not look back as he trudged through the sand. Suddenly, his right leg felt as if it were in a vice, and he kicked with his left until the ground wrapped itself around both legs. His legs were swallowed up first, then he was pulled down into the beach itself. He screamed until his head was pulled under and his throat filled with sand.

He was dragged deeper and felt himself being dragged horizontally through the sand as it scraped against his skin like coarse sandpaper. Just as he thought he was going to suffocate, his head emerged into open air. He coughed mouthfuls of sand and gasped for breath. He still could not move most of his body, and though he blinked his eyes, he could see nothing but darkness. The sand stopped moving, but the weight of it told him he was still buried from the neck down. His right arm throbbed and burned, having been pulled from the sling and the open wound filled with sand. He wiggled his left shoulder, then more of his arm until it was free. He touched his face, brushing sand and rubbing his eyes, then reached up only to jam his fingers on hardwood .

He was inside the upside-down hull of the boat that the beach had swallowed. Pounding on the hull felt as solid as rock with the weight of the entire beach above it. There was no telling how deep he was, or how much air he had in his underground bubble. His screams echoed in the deathly silent space as he scraped and punched the boat and his cries for help turned to sobs.

The weight of the beach around his chest made it hard to catch his breath. He began hyperventilating—suffocating. His left arm grew too weak to continue clawing and his head started pounding. Time passed in a haze, and the pure blackness morphed into swirls of color and flashes of light like snow. His heartbeat rang in his ears like distant drums and lulled him into somewhere between madness and sleep.

Tunwood Landing. The inn was warm and so was the bed he laid in. The woman was there again—Clara was her name. She lay next to Edward, naked, one hand on his chest and the other tucked under a pillow as she stared at him. Not often, but sometimes his stays at the inn ended this way; perhaps the lonely sailor at the bar and the widow who served him felt like sleeping alone again, or perhaps it was something more that Edward never stayed around long enough to explore.

*Had she been awake long?* Edward thought to himself.

"No, I've only just stirred," she said. "You were talking in your sleep."

*I had a dreadful dream.*

"I could tell." She was standing now, fully dressed, and staring out the window towards the ocean. "It is morning. Must you leave?"

*I must. We set sail soon, I believe.*

"Shame. I would be glad if you were to stay with me."

Edward looked at her closer now. Something was wrong. Something about her face. Suddenly, Edward realized he was dreaming, and the room around them fell away. It was just the woman now, standing over his bed looking down at him. He remembered her and had dreamed about her often, but it never occurred to him until now that he could not remember the color of her eyes.

When Edward awoke it was dusk, and the island had brought him back to the surface. He was laying inside the boat, now filled with sand to the brim with him nestled on top of it. He looked out to the water and saw no boat. Whether they had come to investigate or not, they were gone now. Edward groaned and rolled his head back to the island. A figure stood next to the boat looking down at him.

Her pale skin was made of sand, the individual grains carefully separated and segregated into gradients of color to give the illusion of skin tone. The creases of her belly button and the shape of her areolas were made of a darker sand. Her lips were smooth clay, and her hair was fibers from plants and trees woven together. Her eyes were empty sockets sunken into the figure's skull, leaving it expressionless and soulless.

Edward stared into the empty holes. "What are you?" he asked.

The figure did not move for a while, long enough that Edward was not sure if it could. Then, the figure's clay lips pulled apart as it figured out how to work them. Its neck tilted slightly as the mouth continued to move and twist into shapes foreign to it. Suddenly, countless sounds from the island behind the figure grew louder and louder, overlapping and blending while the figure's silent mouth moved along to the sound.

"...C-c-c-c-" the sound of stones and sea shells clanging together, "Llll-" the twisting of wooden branches, "A-a-a-a-" the bending of whole trees, straining the wood. The sounds became more defined as the figure continued mouthing, "Claaaraaa."

"You're nothing of the like," Edward seethed. "You are a demon is what you are! Leave me be!"

Edward swiped at the figure, his hand passed through a section of her torso sending sand, sticks and stones flying, but the section filled itself in with more sand. He ran towards the water until his feet became trapped and he collapsed on top of his bad arm. The broken bones shifted and he struggled to breathe through the pain. Sitting up, he pulled the sleeve back to inspect his arm. The familiar sickly-sweet smell of infection stung his nostrils.

The figure slid towards him; its legs were motionless as it glided on the surface of the sand. It gripped his wrist and pushed his arm into the sand with such force he feared it would dislocate his shoulder. Edward gasped for air as the pain stole his breath.

The sand began swirling like a viscous whirlpool around his arm, grinding against his skin. It cut through his flesh, spinning faster until the friction burned him. Edward screamed and flailed and kicked at the figure, but any time he hit it, the sand would swipe away in chunks only to be filled back in.

The swirling stopped and the creature released Edward's arm. He pulled it from the sand to find a stump where his elbow should have extended, the end was muddy with bloody clods of sand and charred flesh. Shock took Edward back into unconsciousness as the figure stayed hovering over him, staring down at him with its empty eye sockets.

Edward did not dream of Tunwood Landing, but when he woke, he was on the beach. A mound of sand meant to look like Clara lay next to him with one arm resting on his chest, but the heap of sand was inanimate — a sculpted sand castle in the mere shape of a beautiful woman he once knew. He sat up and her arm lost its shape as it sifted into loose sand.

"M-m-must you leave?"

Edward said nothing. He stepped on her chest which caved in easily as he walked towards the boat. He took off his shirt, tied the sleeve of the shirt to the sleeve of his jacket, and tied the other sleeve into a noose. The boat was laid under a leaning palm, so he stepped up into the boat and stood up on the seat to fling the noose over the palm and tie it in place. He put the noose around his neck and looked out to the ocean as he readied himself. The beach stirred, and halfway between Edward and the water the Clara figure rose from the ground like the sails of a ship rising over a horizon. The figure stared at Edward with empty eyes as he stepped off the boat. The noose pulled tight against his throat and he resisted the urge to thrash. The beach stirred and the tree Edward hung from creaked. The tree's roots were pushed up, emerging from the sand on one side, and Edward was lowered safely back on the beach.

He sat back up, looked around, and found the sharp rock he had used to hack open coconuts. He picked it up and turned it around in his hand before picking the sharpest side. He lined it up to his temple, and swung the rock towards his head. Just before making contact, the rock burst into sand and cascaded pointlessly over him.

Clara rose from the sand next to him and stared out into the ocean with him. She rested her head on his shoulder. It was cold, her hair and skin itched him but he did not shake her off. The island rumbled behind him, "I would be g-g-glad if you were to stay with me."

# THE LAST TREE NYMPH
## By Janessa Keeling

WHEN I FOUND MY sisters slaughtered in their human shapes, golden sap staining garments and spilling from deadly wounds, their vacant eyes staring unseeing at the sky and sun, I wept. I did not understand why the humans would come with axes for my family. We'd done nothing but help them understand the plants and the seasons—when to place seeds and how to plant them so a healthy symbiotic relationship would form. When to leave the earth to heal for a season.

Afraid the humans would return, I surrendered my human form. As a billowing willow, the indescribable pain of losing everyone I loved was dulled, and I was hidden in plain sight. It was so long ago that I no longer remember how to resume my human form. The humans rush past me on their two little flesh stumps. They cling to weapons of murder, but not the kind that could chop through my bark.

They come in drops, like rainwater collecting in my leaves before splashing to the ground.

Then they come in a flood, sunlight winking a message off breast plates: Run.

I dare not move. If they believe I am a tree they may leave me be, if they see me move they will come with axes.

When I planted my roots, I stood alone and was, if not happy, content. A collection of huts burst from the ground. At first, remembering my sisters and their joy for life, I was glad for the companionship. Children played near the base of my trunk and climbed my branches, their mothers resting in my shade.

The ebb and flow of humans was a tide that kept me content. I allowed myself to forget human greed, the same greed that consumed my sisters. Soon, the tide of humans becomes a wave. They grow faster than bamboo, adapting better than Venus Flytraps—with a hunger twice as ravenous.

Smoke billows. Heat-licking flames pick at my sides.

I rip myself from the earth, rending dirt and rock to free myself. Leagues pass—and as I go—I sprinkle seeds in hopes that a single sprout will take root. That I will not be the last.

Near thirst-quenching water, I find a new home.

Cool protective humus, untouched and full of food. Soft topsoil, crawling with worms. Shifting sand and silt. Subsoil. I drop more seeds.

Thousands of times the sun casts her glorious rays across me and the moon shines his illuminating glimmer across the river.

A single seed takes root and sprouts, roots reaching deeper and tangling with my own. Soon she will open her eyes and I will no longer be alone.

A collection of huts burst from the ground.

# ALL THINGS DEAD
## By Marília Bonelli

THE SICKLY SWEET SCENT of death brushed against my mind.

I wiggled my fingertips, spreading my senses. The living surrounded me with their ridiculous fear and ravenous hatred. Even the log my arms and legs were bound to was not yet dead, a very green sprout rubbing against my ankles.

From the other side of the small bridge, the somber voice grew louder. "…unto the water as her grave…"

Dark waters rippled below. Whatever happened to burning witches at the stake?

Tendrils of my power found something small nearby. Too small to be even a baby. Not that anyone would leave a dead child on the street.

"…for the crimes of witchcraft…" the priest droned on.

Crime? All I had done was make use of a dead donkey to pull my cart.

"The abomination called forth my brother from his grave!" The man's shout distracted me enough that I looked at him. Even though my arms and legs were tied, he flinched when our eyes met.

Idiot. My magic was for the dead. No living thing would be touched by it. I was sure I'd never seen his ugly face, much less disturbed any brother he'd had.

"She brought forth a plague of locusts!" another man shouted from the crowd.

Now that was new.

My left hand started going numb from where the rope dug into my arm, and I tried shifting it. The log shook slightly, dangerously close to falling over the side of the bridge and into the river. Cold seeped from my heart to every inch of skin. I did not want to die like this.

Focusing on the small dead thing nearby, I sent out part of my awareness to it. Voices sank into the background, replaced by the burning heat of a stone bed under the midday sun. The rat raised its cracked head, stiff paws lifting it from the road.

Quickly, it ran towards the bridge. Through its dried eyes, I saw myself tied to the log that looked like a giant monstrosity to the little creature.

The rat weaved through the crowd. Its sharp teeth were still intact, perhaps sharp enough to cut through ropes.

A child shrieked when the rat ran between his legs. My little would-be savior scurried past the priest and the guards. As it approached the log, a sharp impact landed on its side, and it flew off the bridge.

Its body fell into the water a second before I could pull back my mind. The burning pain flashed through my own body. I shivered, clenching my teeth not to scream.

If having a surrogate dipped in water hurt that much, I could only imagine how much more it would hurt when my own body was submerged.

No, not like this. Not for nothing but prejudice and hatred.

I spread my mind as far as my power allowed. Almost at the edge of my reach, between dead leaves and bug carcasses, I felt a larger death. A deer, maybe. I latched onto it.

My mind dove into the connection to the death in the woods. Cool earth embraced me, falsely soothing my sunburned skin.

The body was almost the same size as mine. It pushed against the soft earth of its shallow grave with the unnatural movements of a puppet. Living things crawled inside it, repulsive in how they disturbed the cold comfort of death.

I shuddered. But life is necessary even in death.

Hands burst from the soil, pushing the broken body up from the dead leaves.

A fleeting smile came as the girl stood on rotting legs and started running.

There was a reason one did not attack a deathweaver near a cemetery.

When the corpse emerged from the woods, screams erupted from the gathered crowd. Panic spread among the gawking onlookers. They moved like a flock of sparrows being charged by a falcon.

The priest squealed his prayers from behind a wall of city guards. Only two soldiers were brave enough to remain in the girl's path.

The girl dodged the first startled soldier as he pulled out his sword. She threw a clump of dead leaves and dirt from her clenched hands at the other soldier's face.

One of the terrified fools bumped into my log. It spun and teetered on the edge of the bridge, leaning over the water as if in slow motion.

From the girl's dead eyes, I watched the log and my body lean forward. With my own, I could see only the water awaiting me below.

The girl reached for my bound hands, her movements fueled by my despair. But not even in life had this girl enough strength to stop the log from falling. Our fingertips, both cold and moist—mine from sweat, hers from morning dew—brushed against each other.

I left my own self behind and, through dead eyes, watched my empty corpse fall into the black river.

The guards approached cautiously.

I bolted on unfamiliar legs, aiming for the woods.

"The witch took my daughter!" a woman wailed.

A tinge of pity snuck into my heart, but not enough to regret my choice. I wouldn't have to ride this wretched corpse if they hadn't drowned my body in the river.

The crowd parted in waves while the guards grew bolder in their chase, closing in.

Subconsciously, my eyes were drawn to one haunted expression that stood out from the rest. Upon seeing this body, there was no surprise on the young guard's face—only fear. A different kind of fear.

The girl's dead eyes locked onto his, and I could not pull away. Hatred bubbled and blistered to the surface from the icy depths of what remained of her soul. Remnants of who she had been came as shards of memory, cutting and painful like ice daggers stabbing into my thoughts.

In that one everlasting second, each fragment faded away like ice melting in the sweltering sun. The last shard melted to reveal that soldier's face as his hands pulled away from her neck. The memory of the last thing she'd ever seen vanished into nothingness, lost forever along with her self, and her life.

My voice, forever gone, would not come.

I smiled, putrid flesh and all, a half-gnawed off finger pointing at him.

"The abomination chose him!"

"He's with the witch!"

"Get him!"

I could have laughed. It wasn't what I intended, but I'd take it.

The sudden outburst of chaos as the villagers swarmed the guard allowed me to slip away from my pursuers. It would not be the death his victim wanted of him, but it would be a death.

Decaying feet sank into equally decaying leaves as the woods welcomed me with the familiar intermingling of life and death. Patches of dead things brushed against my mind here and there, but nothing that would be faster than this girl.

Matted hair and rotting flesh flapped in the wind as I raced along the riverbank. Shouts and thundering footsteps gave chase.

A little further downstream, the river would snake between large rocks before feeding into a waterfall. It would be my best chance at crossing the river towards Glenmaerhen, the forest of the damned, where the bloodiest battle of the last war was fought.

When I reached the cliff's edge, the water level was higher than expected. I'd forgotten the recent rains.

A log—not *my* log—was nestled between two larger rocks, acting as a small bridge. Perhaps my body would eventually end up here as well.

"There she is!"

Unwilling to jump to a painful death in the lake below, I scrambled onto the driest rocks. Slimy hands left a trail of decaying flesh upon the scorching stones and rough bark.

Splashes of water struck my face and arms like boiling oil.

After I'd used it to cross the gap between boulders, I rested a hand on the log, commanding it to break. Long dead and battered by the sun and water, it cracked and sputtered, then washed away with the current.

I threw myself from the last rock towards the shore. The left foot landed in the water while the body, worn and decayed, collapsed onto a mat of pebbles.

My soul was dipped in flames. The dead mouth opened in a silent scream.

I dug the fingertips into the ground to avoid sliding back into the water.

Shouts grew nearer.

I dragged the left leg out of the river. The foot was lost to the water. More of the leg would soon be gone.

Boots scraped along rocks on the other margin.

Underneath the blazing sun, something light and scarred jutted out from the ground between larger rocks.

Driftwood?

Even to senses dulled by this unfamiliar shell, the scent of death was too strong to be tree remnants.

Splashes encompassed a shout as one of my pursuers fell into the water—pity it wouldn't burn him.

A large ribcage came into view. Its insides long devoured and skin gone, most of what remained were bones.

I lunged and grasped a hoof.

The girl's corpse, vacant, collapsed like a broken doll.

Unsteadily, the pale horse rose.

The guards' voices grew louder.

I ran.

No, I galloped.

Fast.

*Faster!*

Wind howled along its skeleton as I left the river behind.

The scent of death wafted from among the trees as I reached their shade.

I was safe.

The forest of the damned did not lack dead things. And what was dead was mine.

# CHERRY BLOSSOM TEA
## By Chris Vannes

HELLO THERE!

I'm sorry, didn't mean to startle you. Was a bit surprised myself. We don't get many visitors, up here in our high valley.

Yes, I said 'we.' Did you think it was just me, an old man all alone in this fair green hollow between the mountains? No, young stranger, I may be alone, but I'm never lonely. You can meet Mother and my brother later. And look, here come my friends now. I'm sure *they* weren't surprised to see you. Probably picked up your scent an hour ago.

Guess you've never seen a dire wolf up close before? Ah, don't worry. They rarely bite, not unless I ask them to. And there's no need for that, is there? You didn't bring any malice to our valley, did you? Any dark intentions?

I thought not.

The wolves are just a mite excited. We get so few visitors. Some seekers, some vagrants, the occasional wandering hero. It's been…what? Six years since the last one I can recall.

But that's to be expected, I suppose. Rarer than hen's teeth, we humans are, since the Flowering. Reminds me of a riddle even older than I am: if a tree grows in the forest, blossoms and sways in the wind, carpets the ground with leaves for a hundred years, then finally falls to make room for another, and there's not a single human alive to see it...was the tree still beautiful?

Ha! Made you think, didn't I? It used to be a harder question. Back in my day, we were so certain that human sentience was the only kind. That we were the only creatures that could think, or speak, or build. The only ones that could look at a tree and call it 'beautiful.'

I was a man of science myself, once. A botanist. We dissected the world, mapped and measured all the plants and trees and birds and fishes, made whole taxonomies of life just so we could put humans at the top and label everything else 'inferior.'

You look a mite confused, young stranger. You haven't the foggiest idea what I'm talking about, have you?

Well, yes, 'hen's teeth' was just an expression back then. Ironic how that one turned out. But you've not heard the tale of the Flowering? My, my, you *are* young. Have I got a story for you, my new friend!

Before that, though — there's no need for us to stand around yammering in the meadow. You look bone-tired. Thirsty, too, I'll wager. It's quite a climb, up over yon pass to find your way in here. Let's get you inside. Out of this wind.

It's this way, just behind these rocks...here we are. Down the stairs and to your left. Mind your head there.

This place? It used to be what we called a research station. Climate change monitoring and such. Back before it all started, a hundred years ago and more. You might not know it, but humans were once convinced we were ruining the environment. What with our teeming cities, and our digging for minerals, and our factories and machines belching clouds of poison.

"Destroying the Earth," some said! I believed it myself at the time. You could call that ironic, too. But somehow, 'ironic' doesn't seem like a big enough word to cover how wrong we all were.

I'm getting ahead of myself. Where are my manners? You must be weary from all that walking. And I bet the wind cuts right through those rags you're wearing; you must be chilled to the bone. Set your things down and have a seat. Let me make you something hot to drink. It'll take just a moment...

Here, try this. It's called 'tea.' Not exactly the same as what we used to call tea, but who's going to complain? This one's my own specialty. Made from cherry blossoms, right here in the valley.

I suppose it is bitter. Sorry about that. I used to love honey in my tea. It was sweet, a kind of liquid sugar we harvested from beehives. Well, after all the bees died, no one had honey in their tea for decades, because there just weren't any hives. Now the bees are back, but it's not worth your life to approach the colony. Have you seen the size of them? The air is so much richer now, all that carbon and oxygen. Bees used to be the size of your fingernail, not your fist.

I'm probably the only one that remembers the old bees.

Or honey.

Or tea, for that matter.

Well, Mother remembers, of course, but she remembers *everything*. So that hardly counts.

Now you know about tea, too. Go ahead, finish it up. That's right.

Where was I? Ah yes, the Flowering. And irony.

All those people running around. Twelve billion of us by the end, can you imagine? A third of the planet covered with our cities. Another third taken up with trying to grow enough food for all those bellies. Every other living thing on the planet squeezed into that last unwanted third, or extinct, or hiding in the cracks and shadows of our cities.

And we had machines. My word, we had machines! Machines for food and machines for work. Machines that would carry you across the continent in a week on the ground or a couple of hours in the sky. Even machines for thinking. Such pride we had, knowing we were the smartest and cleverest beings in creation, and what did we do? Went and built machines to do the thinking for us, so we didn't have to bother.

Those machines were thirsty, too. Not for drink, but for energy. A relentless thirst.

There were warnings, of course. For a century, we heard that we were wrecking the environment: poisoning the water with our industrial waste, killing the forests for farmland, heating up the climate with petroleum fumes. It was all true, and plain as daylight. It was just how humans were, though. An inevitable part of 'progress,' and anyway who could stop it?

Ha! That was the wrong question. The 'who' part, that is.

Let me try a little perspective. Took you a good hour to walk from the ridgeline over yonder down into the valley, I bet? A couple of thousand steps until you met me?

Imagine that walk is the whole history of life on Earth. From the Cambrian Explosion, half a billion years ago, up to today.

On your walk through history, you'd see ice ages and meteor strikes, glaciers advancing and then retreating, mountains pushed up out of the sea. The magnetic poles would switch polarity every couple of paces. But you wouldn't see anything that looks even slightly human until, oh, about twenty steps before you saw me. And what we called the Anthropocene, ten thousand years of human civilization, well, that's just the blink of an eye. About the width of your finger. Or an old-fashioned honey bee.

If everything you knew was what you could see during that half a breath, that one last step before I found you—how deeply would you understand this valley? Well, that's about how well we understood Her. The *real* Mother Earth. Gaia.

It all started with the flowers. A season like no one had known before — everything in bloom at once. Flowers never before seen by man growing through cracks in the pavement. Blooming vines on every bridge and tower. Blossoms bursting through the farm fields, choking out the corn. Golden clouds of pollen in the sky, golden streams in the rivers. For one precious month, the whole world was a garden. An Eden of ravishing beauty and riotous color.

If you ask me, Mother Earth intended all that beauty as a message. A promise that what was coming next was not a punishment but a rebirth. An end to the experiment of individual, selfish human beings with isolated minds; a transition to a higher level of awareness. One where we are joined with the Mother, the greater consciousness of Earth that had been there all along.

My brother actually discovered the first clue. Studying the strange new wildflowers up here in the meadow, he made a curious observation. A new kind of molecule was present in the pollen and petals of every single species he examined. Nanocytes, he called them. Molecules never seen before in nature, crafted anew by Mother Earth from both carbon and silicon. More irony for you: the basic element of life and the basic element of our beloved thinking machines fused into what we called a "semiconductor." One with some quite, ah, *unique* properties.

You see, my brother found that the nanocytes had receptors perfectly suited for clinging to neurons in the human brain. Twelve billion people, breathing them in every day for a month, a bit confused about all the flowers but otherwise going about their business. While the harmless-seeming pollen went about its own business, making copies of those twelve billion minds. Carbon copies, you might say - ha!

Sorry. That was a joke. One that, again, no one but me remembers.

One beautiful month—and then Mother Earth showed us what true power looks like. Hard power, like walls of water scouring the islands clean. Soft power, like the roots of long-dormant trees rupturing foundations, kudzu claiming the skyscrapers. After ten thousand years, our equilibrium was punctuated, and things happened faster than we knew was possible.

Twelve billion humans learned the hard way that the Earth was in no danger from us. Quite the opposite. She taught us what thirst *really* looks like. Twelve billion humans, that's about sixty billion liters of blood. A mere drop compared to the ocean, but Mother Earth drank it eagerly, all the same.

There's some more of that irony I mentioned earlier.

Along with all that blood, She drank the nanocytes. A record of every human alive at the time. Now they're one with Gaia, archived in the great system memory of Earth. Where they can't do any more harm. Who needs thinking machines when every plant and tree is part of a single mind, part of the Mother?

I'm rambling again. Pardon my manners. Like I said, we get so few visitors. Come, walk with me a bit. I want to show you something in the meadow.

Turns out the nanocytes weren't just for recording. The chosen few survivors – we can hear Her now. She speaks to us! I was one of the first to listen, maybe the very first. My brother always wore a mask in his laboratory, but I wasn't so careful outside. So when I first heard Mother's voice, he thought I was losing my mind.

He wasn't entirely wrong. My mind was becoming part of a much larger one. Part of Gaia.

And the first task Mother Earth demanded of me was by far the hardest.

Ah, here we are. The heart of the valley. Have you ever seen a tree this perfect? Called a weeping cherry. Aren't the blossoms lovely? Standing here in the afternoon breeze while they swirl around you must be just how Adam felt in the Garden once upon a time.

That first week of the cataclysm, two of my favorite places in the world were wiped clean off the map. A thousand-year tsunami for Tokyo; hurricane and fire for Washington DC. Two cities famous for their cherry trees, all but gone in three days. This might be the last one now. Who knows.

Anyway, back to the story. Mother told me she required a sacrifice. To prove that I was committed to the rebirth. Worthy to to be an acolyte of the Flowering.

My brother couldn't understand it, poor soul. He didn't have enough nanocytes in his system yet. I had to tie him down while the roots took hold of him. Had to cover his mouth—he wouldn't stop screaming at me. Until the trunk grew up around him. Took just a couple of days. Mother can move pretty quick when She needs to.

My brother, he understands everything now. Right here—that's his toenail. You can still just about see his face, up here. His body's part of the tree, his mind part of the Mother. Just like those twelve billion other minds. I'll finally join him once my task is done. When no more humans are left to mess things up again.

NO! You can't leave!

I do apologize. Sometimes I forget my own strength. Another side effect of the nanocytes. A blessing from Mother.

But you won't be running anywhere now, not with that broken leg. I gave my own brother up to Gaia. Wouldn't hardly be fair to give you a pass. Not fair at all.

No, I'm not going to kill you. The nanocytes need to gather your story, merge it with Gaia. Then you'll live forever. There won't be any more need for that body. You just lie down right here with these roots, now. Let all that carbon and silicon do its job.

What nanocytes? Why, the ones in the tea, of course. Made from the blossoms of this very tree. The Mother Tree.

Can you hear Her voice yet?

Don't worry. You will.

# THE ALCHEMIST
## By V. George

ALCHEMISTS HAVE LONG UNDERSTOOD that the human body is a balance of the four humors, just as the natural world is a balance of the four elements. Yellow bile, black bile, sanguine, and phlegm—imbalances in these four lead to a spectrum of maladies or even differences in temperaments.

Prince Junius was a choleric man, which meant he naturally brimmed with yellow bile and a fiery spirit. He cursed and sputtered like a dampened fire as he was dragged off his horse and into his tent. No amount of incense could smother the heady stench of sweat and rot that followed him.

"My damned arm!" he yelled as he fell clumsily onto his cot. Damp copper hair clung to his forehead. "You have to heal my damned arm!"

Emery, the newly appointed Master Alchemist who possessed a particularly melancholy spirit in his own professional estimation, peeled the vile bandages from the prince's stump. "When they cut off your arm, they divested you of equal amounts of the humors. Amputation creates no imbalance for me to restore."

"I'm not asking you to regrow me an arm, you imbecile," the prince roared. "I'm asking you to reattach my own!"

A lanky boy no older than twenty, the prince's footman, placed a contorted arm on a cushion at the prince's foot. The forearm was crushed from where a horse must have trampled it into the earth. The skin was gray beneath blotchy mud, and a flash of white humerus protruded from the end.

Emery paused. He had reattached fingers and hands by the dozens. So many fingers and hands were lost in battle that soldiers brought them back in sacks alongside belt buckles and buttons, which they offered as pay. As though Emery were interested in turning their bloodied metal into gold after the tedious work of reattaching their digits. All the same, Emery made the best of their spoils of muddy limbs and scraps, and the soldiers often wound up with a different hand or finger than they started with.

But Emery had never heard of an alchemist replacing such a large or mutilated limb. He would have to rebalance the humors within the dead limb before he could even attempt it. Such a thing was closer to necromancy than alchemy, and his mind spun with the impossibility.

"It's in ruins," he said as neutrally as possible to test the expectations of the volatile prince.

The prince's temper rose. "I lost my arm, not my eye, you idiot! I can see that it's in ruins! That's why you must heal it first! What is a prince without his sword arm?"

Emery had heard the whispers of the soldiers—heard rumors the prince's arm had fallen in the mud—long before the prince was dragged back from the front line. Some hoped the loss would humble the prince into halting his conquest so they could at least hold camp over the winter months. Others hoped the prince's thirst for new land would be sated now that his arm had soaked in foreign mud and that the humility would drive him to retreat.

The soldiers inside Emery's wounded tents, the bitterest ones who also left trampled pieces of themselves on the battlefield, openly prayed the prince would burn with sepsis.

Emery wasn't supposed to wish for sepsis in anyone. He had sworn an oath to do no harm, no matter who his patient was.

But did that mean he had to restore the prince's sword arm? Did his oath extend to a dead chunk of flesh? What if the soldiers were right, and his crusade would halt without it?

"I've never healed a detached arm before," Emery said cautiously as he resumed peeling the bandages from the prince's stump. "Your arm is soaked in earth; no doubt it is likewise overrun with black bile. I can try to restore your arm, but I'm not sure it would be wise to reattach it."

The prince was not satisfied with Emery's misgivings. "By all the gods, I wish Abbott were still here! Abbott had a mind for war; he would understand the obvious importance of a sword arm. How do you suppose a man rallies his armies? Do you suppose he urges them to charge by shrugging his stumped shoulder? You are a fool with no understanding of war."

Emery's former master, Master Alchemist Abbott, was a sanguine man notorious for his many fixations. He would often enter a room in the middle of a boisterous rant, such as about how he discovered wild ginger was hotter than the domesticated variety and thus better for improving the wet and cold humors. He was obsessed with alchemizing an element so pure it could puncture the soul. Prince Junius, who was likewise interested in such an element that may be used as a weapon, thus patronized Master Abbott. When the prince set out to conquer the neighboring city-states, Abbott raved about his excitement at harvesting rare ingredients and spoils in the countryside. He packed his and Emery's cart not with rations but with empty glasses and vials that jostled merrily as they strayed from the roads and onto ever rougher paths.

Master Abbott was shot straight through the neck in the first ambush. Emery succeeded him as Master Alchemist and now had seen the true, miserable spoils of war. Bags of fingers and buckles. Tents upon tents of the dying. It was bitter moments like these, the air heady with incense and rot, that Emery knew his teacher was the fool with no understanding of war.

"Alchemy is not a tool for war." Emery peeled back the last layer with less finesse, and the prince drew a seething breath that stopped any further speaking. His stump was black, crusted with sweat and blood. Most concerning of all, the stump was dry and cool. A choleric man should run hot and dry. "It's soaked in black bile. We need to leach it out tonight."

Black bile would manifest as sepsis, like the soldiers prayed for.

"And my arm?"

"I'll work on that as soon as I've done what I can for you."

The prince released a fresh string of curses, but Emery ignored him as he rifled through his trunk of dwindling resources. It would be challenging to treat both a wound and an entire arm overrun with black bile, with both requiring cures that restored heat and moisture. Not to mention, it was September and Virgo, an earth sign, was in full effect. As black bile was the humor associated with earth, the stars would dampen any efforts to lessen black bile.

Emery started by pouring a vial of honey, which was considered warm and wet, into a large poultice bowl. Next, he added apple vinegar to increase the warmth of the concoction, but not so much that the prince would leap off his cot in pain and order the alchemist killed on the spot.

Would there be enough to cure both the stump and the arm? The prince would certainly expect to see his arm steeping in the same poultice as his stump, considering Emery already said both were overrun with black bile.

Emery opened his box of root herbs, made of light pine to promote dryness and keep them out of the sun. Ginger was both hot and dry, but his supplies were running low now that the ginger lay dormant under the earth in the late summer. Even so, Emery plucked the last three pieces of dried ginger from the pine box, each the size of a knuckle.

He was about to close the box when his eye caught on the ginseng root. While ginger was hot and dry, ginseng was cold and dry. But when ground into a powder, ginger and ginseng would look the same.

"Is this the first you've seen your own cursed plants? Get on with it, boy."

Resolved, Emery split the vinegar honey into two glasses. He ground the ginger into a powder and mixed it into one, and for the other he ground and mixed in the ginseng. Emery raised each glass to a candle. They were identical, like clouded honey. The first cure would promote heat and moisture, thus abating black bile. The second was a mixture of warm and wet honey and dry and cool ginseng, and was neutralized into doing nothing. A placebo at best.

The footman had drawn close, watching Emery compare the bottles in the candlelight. Emery turned to him. "The poultices are very similar, but it's extremely important that you lather this one --" Emery passed him the first bottle "-- on his stump and this one- -" Emery passed him the second bottle "-- on the arm. You'll need to reapply every hour, and you can use my hourglass to keep track."

At first Emery worried the boy would ask him for the reason for the distinction, but the footman was sweating as though it were his arm cut off and not his prince's. His eyes were wide in terror, and his lips silently repeated the instructions like a prayer.

The prince hadn't paid any attention to the instructions. He was flailing his head back and forth on his cot, cursing and seething with rage.

Emery nearly slipped out of the tent before the prince caught sight of him. "Alchemist," he called out. "You best pray this works. You'll reattach my sword arm tomorrow, or you'll be replacing it with your own."

The threat washed over Emery. The prince would take his arm. In the place where Emery once felt fear of the prince, Emery could only muster a deep exhaustion.

Emery let the tent flap close behind him.

He still had a long night ahead of him. There were soldiers that had come back with the prince in need of healing, and a threat from the prince could not distract him from his obligations to the wounded.

The tents on the fringe of the base were overrun with the sick and wounded. As soon as he returned to them, Emery was greeted with a cacophony of coughing and wailing. The butcher was already hard at work amputating mutilated limbs and clipping back bone in limbs already lost on the battlefield.

Would the butcher take his arm tomorrow to give to the prince? Emery distracted himself by making poultices for fevers and seeping wounds. Wounds like those that were full of sanguine humors, hot and wet, alleviated by teas of dehydrated citruses and crushed mint, which were dry and cold.

When the prince took his arm, could Emery then return home? Would he pay such a price for freedom from the choleric prince's campaign?

Emery arrived at the foot of the sickest of his patients, a broad soldier who suffered burns. Despite the pain, he smiled as Emery approached. A phlegmatic man, certainly, with a spirit of water and a calm disposition. "Master Alchemist, I can't say I'm glad to see you in these circumstances, but I'm glad to see you all the same."

Emery pulled back his blankets to assess the burden of his burns. Fire, associated with the choleric humor, always burned away the flesh and left nothing but watery phlegmon. Already, bland water soaked through his bandages. Emery grimaced. The entire left half of the man's body was covered in burns. He wouldn't make it through the night.

From the watery look in the man's eyes, he knew it too.

"I'll do what I can, but I will focus on relieving your pain," Emery said.

The man nodded, and Emery set to work on an ointment with a base of rose oil and opium, which would bring warmth to his wound but also soothe it.

"You've heard what they are saying, that the prince may stop his campaign now that he's lost his sword arm?" the man asked. "I was on the front lines with him. I saw them bring the arm back. Do you plan on restoring it?"

Emery didn't answer that. He applied a liberal dusting of chamomile and even the last of his precious saffron to the man's burns. This would bring even greater warmth to his wounds, giving them a chance to heal if there were any. Emery doubted he would be practicing alchemy after tomorrow anyway. There was no use in rationing his supplies.

As Emery finished his work, the man smiled again. "Please forgive me, young Master Alchemist. I was only curious. I don't think I will survive long enough to find out for myself. The other soldiers will be furious if you do, but I don't believe it matters if you restore his arm. My brothers forget that the prince is an inherently violent man. It will take a change in his heart, not the loss of his arm, for him to reconsider his warpath."

Emery's heart sank at his wisdom. The soldier was right. Emery acted foolishly on false hopes. Of all people, Emery should know better that the loss of the prince's arm did not change his choleric temperament. Emery's own arm would be on the battlefield, sword in hand, in a few short weeks.

"Maybe not a change in his heart, but a change in his very character, his temperament," Emery said, as realization dawned on him.

The prince needed an alteration of his choleric temperament. Needed his spirit of fire cooled.

The man's eyes were closing slowly. The exhaustion of his injuries and opium absorbed through them no doubt made his eyelids heavy.

"I'll tell you this, I'm obligated by oath to treat the maladies of my patients, but in no part of my oath am I obligated to treat an amputated arm."

The man laughed weakly and then drifted into sleep.

By the time the sun rose on the next day, he had passed on.

Emery returned to the tent of the prince, his heart in his throat. As soon as he pressed into the tent, the rot of the arm struck him before his eyes could adjust to the darkness. A handful of soldiers were already there, the prince's best soldiers. At the center, Prince Junius sat upright in his cot. His copper hair had dried flat to his head, and dark circles pouched under his eyes. He clearly had been awake all night, sweating out the black bile and watching his arm deteriorate.

His arm was little more than a dusky black husk; the skin dried and retracted from his fingernails. The humerus protruding from the end was slick with a vinegar-honey poultice.

"Restrain him," the prince said.

There was no use asking them to wait, so Emery announced instead: "I have a solution."

The soldiers restrained him regardless, but the prince was at least intrigued. "Go on?"

"I'm disappointed the poultice didn't work on the arm. But I've found a better arm to replace it."

"An arm better than my own sword arm?"

"Not better than your original sword arm, but a far more comparable arm and certainly better than mine."

The prince flicked his hand, and the soldiers released him. Knowing the short patience of the prince, Emery asked that they fetch the phlegmatic soldier who had passed in the night as well as the butcher. As soon as the prince laid eyes on the soldier, he smiled with a cruel pleasure. "Indeed, he has much larger arms than yours."

"I have come to understand that the importance of a sword arm is that it should be as intimidating as the sword itself," Emery said. "So it would be best to have an arm that has held a sword before?"

The prince laughed. "Maybe you picked up something from your Master Abbott after all."

With that, the butcher cut the arm of the dead, phlegmatic soldier at the humerus. He cleaned the flesh from the bone so part of it protruded just like the arm, a perfect puzzle piece to insert into the hole of the prince's stump.

All the while, the prince drank heavily to prepare himself

for the procedure. As he became increasingly intoxicated, he commented on the size of his new sword arm, how the forearm would now be bulkier than his old arm. He joked that his shoulders may grow broader to support such an arm and he may have to commission new armor. His soldiers laughed.

Emery prepared the necessary ointments. Normally, he would create an ointment that promoted the dominant humor in the man to whom he was restoring the finger or hand, which in the prince's case would be choleric, fire. But this time, he made an ointment that promoted phlegmon, water. He ground wild moss into cedar ashes, both cool and wet like water. He applied eucalyptus oil until it was a thick paste. He conveniently forgot to use opium in the mixture.

He applied the paste to the end of the arm, including the end of the bone and the raw edges of flesh.

"Master Emery, here I had taken you for a fool; you have surprised me," the prince said as Emery applied the paste to his stump.

Emery silenced him by placing linens in his mouth. "Don't bite your tongue."

Emery had seen the butcher's work and knew he offered no warnings, and so was pleased when the hulking man unceremoniously shoved the sharp humerus into the prince's stump. The prince screamed through the linens in his mouth and nearly leapt off his cot, but the butcher held him down with his other arm.

The butcher grunted in displeasure and pulled the arm back off. He sat down to sand down the humerus a touch more.

The prince spat out the linens and cursed the butcher, cursed

Emery, and cursed all of alchemy in the names of all the gods. Declared he should have them killed.

"Kill us and you'll still have no arm," Emery said with pleasure. "The butcher takes great pride in his work. Do you really want one arm longer than the other?"

But there was no time for the prince to answer before the butcher was on him again, pinning him and again shoving the arm into his stump. The prince wailed like an inferno and vomited.

When the butcher stepped away, Emery stepped into his place. It was his turn. He caked the paste in the crease where choleric flesh met phlegmatic arm, like grout between mosaic tiles. He focused on the scent of eucalyptus and ash, anything to avoid the rot of the old arm and the acidity of vomit filling the tent. At least the prince was now focusing on even breaths rather than cursing them all. Once Emery was satisfied with the application, he wrapped the arm in thick linens.

When it was all said and done, the prince lay shuddering on his cot, his fire spirit reduced to mere coals.

"This better work," he muttered to Emery.

Emery agreed. He needed the arm to assimilate, just not for the reasons the prince expected.

For the rest of autumn, Emery dedicated himself to reapplying the cool ash paste to the prince's wound. After a week, he had sensation in the arm, and in another week, he was able to move his fingers, albeit barely. By the time the leaves had fallen, he had full faculties over the arm and started challenging his soldiers to duels to test it.

In the end, the soldier's wish came true, and they stayed huddled at camp through the winter rather than pushing into new, frozen territories. The prince became a reflective man, often voicing concerns to Master Alchemist Emery that he feared his best soldiers wouldn't understand. Emery nurtured these thoughts, offering phlegmatic eucalyptus creams for aches in his new arm and phlegmatic mint teas for headaches. Spring came, and the soldiers noticed that the prince's ambitions thawed with the ice. He ordered his troops to retreat, thus ending his campaign.

Emery, who left an apprentice and returned as a Master Alchemist, served under Prince Junius all his days. Prince Junius forever sang the praises of his wise alchemist and friend. He would frequently and fondly recall the time he threatened to take Emery's arm. While Master Alchemist Emery would remind the prince he remembered those days much less fondly, he would say he was at least happy to have restored the prince's arm. But he was even more pleased that the same arm never rallied armies to battle because, as Emery maintained, alchemy was not a tool of war.

# AS ABOVE SO BELOW

### A re-telling of the Myth of Persephone

## By Sara Elliott

After a three-year delay, the US has become
the first nation in the world to formally withdraw
from the Paris Climate Agreement.

**NPR, November 4th, 2020**

### EARTH - SUMMER 2021

A BRIEF SWIM OF vertigo hit Persephone as she attempted to open her painted wardrobe and get dressed. It wasn't real. She ought to have remembered that by now. After all, she'd been here nearly a year, and there wasn't much of anything in this place that was what it seemed to be. Not time, which ran in circles, dancing between the present and the past. Nor even physics. What went up didn't always come down. But worst of all, she no longer knew herself. It was as though her memory had been wiped clean.

Perhaps it was those pills. The ones Hades had convinced her to swallow at the party last summer just before her mother called.

Persephone had wandered through the amphitheater, gazing at the rainbow of concertgoers with their spiky hair and razor cuts and long flowing manes. Some of them wore newly screen-printed T-shirts. Others were half-naked. The faint but unmistakable aroma of pot mixed with the scent of sweat.

If it was a madhouse in the parking lot, it was only madder near the stage. At the concession, she ran into Hades. His dark blond hair dipped to hide most of his face as he bent forward to examine a t-shirt. When he looked up and caught sight of her, she couldn't help but notice that he was poetically pale and youthful.

"Hi." She smiled nervously. "I hope I'm not interrupting."

His sculpted lips curved shyly as their eyes met. "No man would ever consider you an interruption." He set the t-shirt back down on the table as he studied her. He'd seen her around Mt. Olympus before, but this was the first time he really had a close look at her. Diamond studs glinted at her pierced brows. Anybody who saw her leaning against the concession in her snug jeans and little white cropped top could see how beautiful (and under-aged) she was. "Hi. I'm Hades."

"Hello. Oh, of course, I should have recognized you." She probably would have, she realized, if she hadn't been so giddy and breathless. "Lord of the Underworld. You're really hot, in case no one's already told you."

"Thanks." He grinned. "First time you've heard this band play?"

"Yeah."

"Me too." Hades continued to stare at her. "Come party with us after the concert."

"Gee, I…" Persephone knew she shouldn't.

"Just for a little while?"

"Well…"

He looked down at their joined hands but didn't release his grip lest she change her mind and slip away. "If I promise to get you home before midnight?"

Persephone tugged at her hand, torn between panic and excitement. She could still hear her mother's voice in her head. What on earth would she think if she knew her daughter was out flirting with the Lord of the Underworld? "I really need to get home. My mom will be worried."

Hades ran his thumb over Persephone's knuckles until her knees went weak. "You can tell her the entire thing was my fault. By the way, what's your name?"

"I'm Persephone. Daughter of Demeter."

"Oh, shit." He winced as he dropped her hand. "I'm sorry, I had no idea. I feel like a complete jerk."

"Why?"

After dragging his fingers through his hair, he let them fall. "The Goddess of Earth's daughter, and here I am making a stupid pass."

"I didn't think it was stupid," she murmured. "See you after the show?"

Two hours later, she found herself sitting in a loud, crowded club on the shadier side of Mt. Olympus. That was where she'd taken the pills. Four of them, to be exact. Hades had called them smart pills. Smart as in artificially intelligent. She could still hear them talking to her sometimes—a strange echoing sound that came from deep inside her belly.

Persephone's phone rang, and she slid her thumb over the green icon.

She'd heard her mother's voice, vague and distant, saying, "*Hello? Hello?*"

Persephone could hardly speak. She imagined her mother in her nightgown in bed, blinking in the dark at the clock.

"Hello?" her mother said again.

"Hello, Mom."

"Where the hell are you, young lady? It's two in the morning?" Over the line, Persephone could hear an engine approaching. Her mother had her on speakerphone. "Your father's here. I'm sure he'll be worried too."

As they listened together to Zeus' footsteps in the next room, Persephone thought about the wealthy, powerful man who never bothered to pay child support or show up for her birthdays, but still managed to find his way to the house, often under dubious pretenses, whenever there was something that he wanted from her mother. "Of course he will…not." She rolled her eyes for emphasis.

"Persephone, don't speak about your father that way."

"Whatever, Mom." Persephone rolled her eyes again. "Anyways, there's nothing to worry about… I'm just having a little fun. I promise I'll be home soon."

"All right, honey," her mother said, her voice growing softer in anticipation of her lover's arrival. "Just don't do anything I wouldn't."

She hung up, thinking it was already too late for that…

As Earth's climate changes, it is impacting extreme weather across the planet. Record-breaking heat waves on land and in the ocean, drenching rains, severe floods, years-long droughts, extreme wildfires, and widespread flooding during hurricanes are all becoming more frequent and more intense.

**NASA, *Vital Signs of the Planet***

## UNDERWORLD,
## JUST AFTER PERSEPHONE'S ARRIVAL

*PILLS – We are a chorus of pills.*
*Smart pills that erase free will*

*Demeter was Persephone's child.*
*One night she got a little wild.*
*Strike that. Persephone was Demeter's child.*
*And now she's been exiled.*

*Not exiled but kidnapped*
*And to this day she's trapped.*

*If she isn't rescued soon*
*The earth may meet its doom.*

*Persephone's mother is mad.*
*And she's made the weather bad.*

*Tornadoes, tsunamis, floods and fires.*
*Life on earth may soon expire.*

*We, the smart pills, know that this is true*
*But we're all controlled by Hades, so whatever can we do?*

## EARTH - WINTER 2021

*"Those damn pills!"* Demeter muttered under her breath as she watched the white-coated back recede from the fluorescent glare of her hospital room. "They tell me I need to be medicated. That I'm not well these days and it's for my own good. But I highly doubt it. Ever since I started taking their so-called medicine, I've been burning up with fever. My oceans are bloated, and my poles are sagging. They've genetically modified my crops and don't even get me started on my stomach acid. Or that terrible gas. Carbon emission is the polite word they use for it around here."

She waved the small paper cup with four wretched pills inside beneath her nose and stared down at them. "If you're as smart as everyone says you are, then *you* tell me how I got here."

*PILLS – You were searching for your daughter*

*Scouring every space*
*For days and days on end*
*Since she vanished without a trace*

"My daughter! Oh, dear gods and goddesses! My daughter!" Demeter's eyes, which, only moments earlier, had been without light, as though someone had taken a tiny brush and painted them gray, now lit with startled brightness. "I must go and find her at once! That is unless…

*PILLS – Unless what?*

"She's dead!" The word dead stuck in Demeter's throat as though she were choking on a grape.

*PILLS – Your daughter isn't dead*
*Just in another world*
*Taken there by Hades*
*To be his special girl*

"Special girl?" Demeter sat bolt upright in her bed, dangerous and glowing with rage, as though the fragile drug-induced haze she'd been in for the past several months had suddenly shattered. "When I get down there, I'll rip his…

*PILLS – My lady, please lay down! The nurse will hear you!*

Demeter listened as the flapping sound of crepe-soled shoes got louder.

"What in heaven's name is going on in here?" Nurse Valerie demanded. It seemed to Demeter that her eyes momentarily popped out of their sockets and flew about the room.

*PILLS – Our patient desires to leave us.*

"Nonsense," said Nurse Valerie. " It's against the rules!"

"Against the rules, my ass!" Demeter blistered with such rage the ceiling fan did little more than slosh heat around the room.

When her lover arrived, half an hour late as usual, the staff could sense the onset of a bruising altercation. Through the wall adjacent to the nursing station, they could just make out the jagged contours of the accusations she hurled at her Zeus.

"This is all your fault!" Demeter hissed. Her Greek furled backward toward its Olympian origins.

"Now hold up just a minute there, Demeter " Zeus stammered.

"Hold up? I most certainly will not hold up! Our baby is missing! If you hadn't been such a sorry excuse for a dad, this never would have happened. And I wouldn't be here, choking on my own carbon in this Godforsaken hell hole!"

*PILLS – Well, actually, Miss…(the pills interrupted Demeter)*
*If you hadn't held Demophone over the fire…*
*Or flooded Pakistan!*

*Or unleashed that hurricane on Cuba!*

*Or caused that tsunami in Japan.*

*You might not be here now.*

*After all, some might view those things as a form of self-harm.*


"Oh, shut up, all of you!" Demeter glared at the pills. "Whose side are you on anyway? And as for you," she shifted her gaze to Zeus, sitting tight-bellied and anxious on the edge of a beige leather chair that made a farting sound whenever he shifted. "You better get your ass straight down to hell and do something about Hades, or else I will!"

No corner of the globe is immune from the devastating consequences of climate change. Rising temperatures fuel environmental degradation, natural disasters, weather extremes, food and water insecurity, economic disruption, conflict, and terrorism. Seas levels are rising, the Arctic is melting, coral reefs are dying, oceans are acidifying, and forests are burning. It is clear that business as usual is not good enough.

**United Nations**


## UNDERWORLD - THE FOLLOWING WEEK


"To the underworld!" Demeter shouted with both feet firmly planted in the toilet bowl. If Zeus wasn't going to man up, she'd just go find her baby by herself. As soon as her fingers tugged at the flapper, she could hear the sands of time whooshing all around her. Who knew there was sand in the toilet bowl. Some of it settled into her collarbones and formed shimmering pools beside her shoulders. When she reached the gates of the land of the dead, she brushed it off, noticing that each tiny grain seemed to take on an other-worldly glow.

Meanwhile, a fat, middle-aged man who resembled a gelatinous mountain stood at the door of Persephone's room, twirling his headphones in insouciant circles.

Persephone's eyes went wide with astonishment when she saw him. "Who the hell are you?"

"Hades. Don't you remember me, babe?"

"Who?"

"Hades. The boy you met at the concert."

"Boy? Concert?" A strange, sweet smell wafted into her memory. Then the sound of music. "Hades! But you don't look anything like him."

"I am. I can prove it." Hades waddled into Persephone's room and pulled up his shirt. His face was bright pink, and he wheezed with every breath, causing an avalanche of flab to jiggle over his waistband. "See? I still have the same tattoo."

Just looking at him made Persephone shudder to imagine what her own reflection might look like. Thankfully, there were no mirrors in the Underworld. Time really did work differently here.

"Eew! Cover that up before I vomit."

"Geez, you don't have to be so harsh." Hades sat in a chair beside

Persephone's bed and waited for air to seep back into his lungs.

"What do you want from me, Hades?"

Hades put one of the thick meat sausages he had for hands on Persephone's thigh, but before he could get so much as a word out, a series of frantic knocks echoed from the ceiling.

"Who's there?" Hades shouted.

"It's Demeter, you bastard! Persephone's mom! Now open up and let me in!"

"Momma!" Persephone squealed. The sound of her mother's voice brought her memories racing back. She shoved Hades aside and raced toward the drawstring that opened the trap door.

"My baby! I was afraid you were dead!" Demeter reached for Persephone and the two of them fell together in a tangle of limbs and tears.

"Not dead. Just stuck in this gods-forsaken hell hole."

"Wait…" Hades looked confused. "Doesn't Zeus usually send Hermes to deal with things like this?"

"Did you honestly think I was going to wait for those two losers to get their shit together and rescue my child? Screw Zeus and Hermes. Screw the entire patriarchy! I'm taking her home. Right now."

"Not so fast!" Hades interjected. "First, you'll have to find your way out of the Underworld."

"Why don't you show me?"

"Because."

"Because why?"

"Because maybe I just don't feel like it."

"Why am I not surprised?" Demeter scowled at Hades. " I'll just have to find a way out myself."

## UNDERWORLD - AN ETERNITY
## YET MOMENTS LATER

The paths of the underworld were twisted and tangled. It wasn't long before Persephone and Demeter found themselves lost in the drunken forest.

"Can I help you ladies?" The disembodied voice came from a peculiar grove of trees, each leaning this way and that.

"Who said that?" Demeter asked.

"We, the trees, of course."

"Can you tell us how to get back to Earth?"

The forest filled with laughter and muffled voices. "Go this way," said one tree, leaning to the right. "No, that way," said another, leaning toward the left.

"Which is it then? This way or that way?"

"It's neither and both." The laughter grew louder again.

"That isn't helpful at all," Demeter snapped. Each time one of the trees spoke, a little cloud of carbon smoke came out of the mouth on its trunk and formed arrows that pointed in random directions.

"We can't help it," said a third. "The permafrost has been melting for years now."

"That's right," a fourth tree added. "And it's gotten us all quite drunk."

Before long, the entire area was filled with so much smoke that Persephone and Demeter could hardly see a thing.

Permafrost thaw is one of the world's most pressing climate problems, already disrupting lifestyles, livelihoods, economies, and ecosystems in the north, and threatening to spill beyond the boundaries of the Arctic as our planet continues to warm.

The Arctic Institute,
Commentary by Brandon M. Lucas,
February 23, 2021

## MEANWHILE, BACK ON EARTH

Zeus lit a cigarette and passed the lighter to Hermes beside him on the couch as they watched the chariot races. Before the first event ended, the two of them had a six-pack apiece. Zeus' phone rang twice, but he let his voicemail do the talking.

*"Dad, it's Persephone. Mom and I are lost in the drunken forest. I need you to come pick us up. Right now!"*

Zeus tossed his phone aside and leaned forward in his seat. The floor beneath him was scattered with crumbs from the pretzels and chips. Rings of smoke curled toward the ceiling.

"Damn it!" He jumped up and shouted as the spectators went wild. Sweaty horses panted and gasped on the screen, just inches from his face, and then crossed the finish line. "We lost!"

The world will likely breach the internationally agreed-upon climate change threshold in about a decade and keep heating to break through the next warming limit around mid-century even with big pollution cuts, artificial intelligence predicts in a new study that's more pessimistic than previous modeling.

NPR, January 2023

## UNDERWORLD, SAME TIME

"We're lost," Demeter grumbled when the last of the smoke finally cleared.

"I called Dad, but he didn't answer."

"It doesn't surprise me. Zeus hasn't been all there these days." The voice came from beneath the surface of the lake. Startled, Persephone gazed into the water. Just below the surface, a bundle of translucent tentacles trailed like a purple cape behind a glowing sack-shaped body.

"Come to think of it, neither have I," said the jellyfish.

"Who are you?"

"My name is Akari," she said. As she spoke, bubbles streamed from her lips, and her noodle-like appendages periodically vanished, sometimes leaving little more behind than a glowing pair of spots that functioned as eyes.

"My mom and I are trying to get back to Earth. Do you think you can help us?"

"Yes," Akari replied. "But speak softly. Otherwise, my bones might collapse." She motioned with her tentacles for the two of them to follow her into the water and then looked deeply into their eyes. "Who are you two?"

"I'm Persephone, and this," she said, shifting her gaze toward her mother, "is my mom, Demeter."

"Ah, so you still know your names."

"We outsmarted the smart pills and tricked them into helping us remember. Now tell me about yourself."

"I'm a mutant jellyfish—one of the few species that can still live in the waters of Lake Acherusian since they got so warm. Most know me around here as the keeper of the bones."

"What sort of bones are they?" Persephone could not imagine that this gelatinous creature had any bones.

"They're the bones of all the species that no longer exist on Earth." Akari swam through the murky shallows and beckoned for Persephone and Demeter to follow her.

Persephone and Demeter nodded and moved through the water as gently as they could until they saw the bones, gleaming in the silt. There were heads and wings and spines and tails.

"Thanks to climate change, more than ever before are going extinct," Akari explained. Whatever is left of them ends up here, in the Underworld. But if their bones crumble before they return to Earth, they're gone forever."

"What is climate change?" Persephone asked.

"You mean to tell me you don't know?" Akira looked startled. "It's the terrible shift in the environment that was caused by the two of you!"

"Are you implying that my mom and I destroyed the environment?"

Akari's body disappeared again, this time leaving only her lips.

"Listen, young lady," she said to Persephone. "I'm not one for arguments. In fact, I rarely ever say a word. But I will say this. You and your mother need to get back to Earth immediately. Otherwise, the planet is doomed."

"But how do we do that?"

"You'll have to find the River Styx."

"What is that?" Persephone wanted to know.

"It's the river that forms the boundary between Earth and the Underworld," Akira explained. "It's a place of timelessness and infinite being, of everywhere and always. It borders on all worlds and has access to everything. You each took one of those pathways when you passed from Earth into the Underworld."

"Are you saying that the River Styx lies *between* Earth and the Underworld?" Persephone asked, realizing quite suddenly that she was shouting, and promptly lowered her voice.

Akira shook her bulbous head. "Not exactly. It's a magical place of non-being. It is everywhere and nowhere all at once. Do you understand what I mean?"

Persephone smiled. "No."

"That's bad," Akira whispered.

"What do you suggest we do?" Demeter asked.

After a considerable silence, Akira replied: "You must find a guide to show you."

The thought of putting her trust in any of the mutants that called this desecrated place home sent shivers down Demeter's spine. Wasn't that how her daughter got herself into this mess in the first place - by trusting Hades? She didn't comment, but Akira heard her thoughts.

"The guidance you seek may well be within."

Neither Persephone nor her mother said anything more. Instead, they followed Akira deeper and deeper into the water until a jolt signaled that they had gone as deep as they could possibly go.

Since they could see nothing at the bottom of the lake, they chose to be still. They could only hope that, by some miracle of fate, they would eventually find their way out again. How long they lay there, floating in the darkness, it was hard to say. Such a calculation was nearly impossible in the eternal night of the lake. But eventually, Persephone began to hear familiar voices coming from her belly. It was the pills again.

*PILLS - If you want to return to earth*
*You must undergo rebirth*
*You'll go home with your mother*
*And the seasons will recover*

*But, because you swallowed us,*
*The pills, four of us to be exact*
*For four months out of the year,*

*You must return to the Underworld.*

Unsure what to do, Persephone woke her mother.

"We'll worry about the details later," Demeter insisted. "Let's just get the hell out of here and go home."

They climbed into the pool of swirling water that had formed at the bottom of the lake. As they did so, the lake and everything else around them vanished.

In that final moment, just before they lost their ability to breathe underwater, they each drew in a deep breath and listened as the sands of time blew in their ears. The current carried them, splashing and spluttering, back to the living world.

*Mom? Mom!* Still sandy and wet and screaming, Persephone found herself back on Earth, in her room, which long, long ago, she'd snuck out of to go to the concert. At first, she didn't recognize her bed, her posters, the tubes of lipstick and blush that still sat open on her nightstand. But when she looked out her window, she remembered where she was.

"Persephone!" Demeter gathered her daughter into her arms. "Don't cry. Everything's okay. We're safe at home."

"How long have I been gone?" Persephone asked.

"Just over a year. When you didn't come home from that concert, I feared the worst. I was half crazy with worry and Zeus refused to help me. So I told him I was done with him for good, and I went down to the Underworld to bring you home myself."

"Thanks, Mom." Outside, the first droplets of spring rain left trails of silver on the window. By the time evening came, the rain had washed the world clean and made it new again. Tiny buds began to open, and the hillsides were upholstered in velvety green.

"Promise me you'll never leave me again?" Demeter asked Persephone.

"Only for the cold months. Four, to be exact."

"If you like," Demeter said, "I could do away with winter."

"No," Persephone replied. "It's my responsibility, and I want to do it. Without winter, the earth couldn't rest, and things would be out of balance again."

"You are right, my dear." Demeter took Persephone's hands. "I can't contain you any more than I could stop the cycle of life. But you keep Hades in line, you hear me? It's the only hope for life on Earth."

With more frequent and extreme weather events…there is no question that the climate crisis is here now…But there is good news: every day, we see more individuals, organizations, businesses, and governments …coming together to mitigate the worst impacts. By working together, we can change course.

**World Wildlife Fund, 2024**

# THE END

## DUBLIN CREATIVE WRITERS

Dublin Creative Writers (DWC) provides a supportive and constructive environment for writers of all genres and experience levels. Our meetings include write-ins, technical/ craft workshops, writing contests, social events, and group critique sessions. We are a registered 501(c)(3) organization.

**To join, visit our Meetup page:**

WWW.MEETUP.COM/DUBLIN-CREATIVE-WRITERS

Subscribe to our blog to receive updates
on our activites and published works:

WWW.DUBLINCREATIVEWRITERS.COM

Find our previous works on AMAZON:

**BROKEN PROMISES: An Anthology**
**DESIDERIUM: An Anthology**
**DEAD OF WINTER: An Anthology**
**UNTOLD STORIES: An Anthology**

# AUTHOR BIOS

*Marília Bonelli* grew up in sunny Natal in northeast Brazil surrounded by far too many cats (or so everyone says). She currently lives in Ohio with her husband and son, though there is a noticeable lack of cats. When real life doesn't get in the way, she likes to write about the characters and worlds trying to crawl out of her head. You can find some of her work at www. mariliabonelli.com

*R.C. Calvio* was born in the same year as Dolly the cloned sheep, Tupac's death, and the signing of the peace treaty for the Peloponnesian War. He has a Master of Clinical Mental Health Counseling, and he uses that knowledge to put his characters in bad situations. When he is not writing, he is hiking with his "everything" beagle and planning misadventures.

*Sara Elliott* has B.A in creative writing from the University of California, San Diego. She just finished her first novel *Valley of the Moon*, the story of a divorced empty nester who finally finds the courage at fifty to live life on her own terms, hopefully due out later this year. When she's not writing Sara enjoys teaching others how to make their own literary magic and teaches creative writing workshops every chance she gets. Follow Sara on Instagram: @thisissaraelliott.

*Gabrielle Gold* started writing in middle school and never stopped. She is featured in two of Dublin Creative Writers' previous anthologies, *Desiderium* and *Untold Stories*. Her songs have earned awards in contests at science fiction and music conventions, and her current major project is a high fantasy quartet. When not writing, she loves singing, enjoying international food, tabletop roleplaying, and talking to her peace lily and Christmas cactus. The plants tolerate her presence well enough.

*Amy Gordon* is the author of numerous books for young readers (*Painting the Rainbow*, *Twenty Gold Falcons*) and her poems have appeared in *The Amsterdam Review*, *The Massachusetts Review* and other journals. She has published two poetry chapbooks and a third is forthcoming. She lives in Western Massachusetts. Find out more about Amy here: https://www.amyagordon.com/

*Valerie George, MD* studied creative writing at Vanderbilt University and is currently a radiology fellow specializing in breast imaging at Ohio State University in Columbus, Ohio. She collects vintage books, especially fairytales, and loves giving new life to the genre with fairytale reimaginings. She has been a member of Dublin Creative Writers since 2020.

*A. Howitt* took riding lessons on an ornery horse who bucked and complained until he got tired, and then just did the work. After twenty years of writing and revising, she goes through similar tantrums when sitting down to her desk. Stickers, dry-erase markers, inspirational magnets, and cute notebooks are part of her ongoing therapy. She writes dark fantasy and has published a handful of short stories. Find her on Facebook A. Howitt

Leslie *"XPLovecat" Horn* has had a lifelong passion for storytelling. She believes it's one of the most important ways to teach, build empathy, and expand creativity. Leslie spends most of her time as a developmental editor and certified book coach for fantasy, sci-fi, and horror writers. When she's not writing, editing, or playing tabletop roleplaying games, Leslie works on her two YouTube channels under her internet name: XPLovecat. Writing Craft & Story Analysis: https://www.youtube.com/@XPLovecatFiction
Tabletop Roleplaying Games: https://www.youtube.com/@XPLovecat

*Janessa Keeling* is currently attending Arcadia University for a Master of Creative Writing. When not writing, Janessa likes to watch her chickens, and work on DIY projects that will never be finished. Her work can be found with Black Hair Press, *Fairy Tale Magazine*, and Word Fire Press.

Roxane Llanque is a German Bolivian writer and filmmaker. Her award-winning short film *Aberration* was selected for The Madrid Human Rights Festival and her micro *The Tell-Tale Present* won the 2023 Outstanding Miniature of World Pride

Australia. Her essays were published in magazines like *BW/DR* and *Stanchion*, her fiction in anthologies like *We Are All Thieves of Somebody's Future, Other Worlds* and *Not Your Papi's Utopia: Latinx Visions of Radical Hope*. She is currently writing her first novel. You can find her on social media at @roxanellanque or at her website https://roxanellanque.com.

*Kelly Matsuura* is an avid short story writer with a focus on fantasy, horror, and literary fiction. Most recently, she has published stories with *Black Hare Press, 100-foot Crow, Metastellar,* and *The Sirens Call Ezine*. Her poetry is featured in *Black Cat Publications* and *The Ravens Quoth Press*. Kelly lives in Nagoya, Japan with her geeky husband. She loves traveling, knitting, cooking, and of course, reading. https://www.facebook.com/writerkmatsuura

*Anna McHugh* was born in Glasgow, Scotland and moved to Australia as a teenager. She did a PhD at Sydney, and a DPhil at Oxford, then returned to Sydney where she trained as a high school teacher. She is now a dog walker. You can read her short pieces at https://thediogenesblog.wordpress.com

*R. A. O'Brien* is a Tasmanian poet and writer of speculative literary fiction. She has a PhD in unconscious learning and degrees in psychology, fine art, and mathematics, and has had work placed or shortlisted in national and international literary competitions. Her writing has appeared or is forthcoming in *The*

*Phare*; *Epiphany*; *Abyss and Apex*; _ACE III_, an anthology of short fiction from Australian emerging writers; and the *International Journal of the Humanities*.

*Dermott O'Malley* is a lover of horror, whiskey, and sometimes, horrible whiskey. He is the author of short stories such as Thread Count, Memoirs of a Mute and West for Its Own Sake. His stories have been published in various anthologies and magazines.

*J. H. Schiller* writes speculative fiction with a flair for the weird and a healthy dose of the absurd. Her short fiction has been featured in several anthologies and digital publications. The first two volumes in her Comedy of Horrors trilogy, *The Witch of Tophet County* and *Playing with Fire*, are available from Podium Publishing. She is a member of the SFWA. Find her online at jhschiller.com.

*Autumn Shah* lives in the suburbs of Columbus, Ohio with her husband, two teenage daughters, and her pandemic doodle, but dreams of one day living abroad. When she's not writing she can be found walking her dog, staying active, studying French, and reading. Her creative nonfiction has appeared in *Toasted Cheese*, *Anomaly* and *Gravel*. Her fiction has won local, Ohio writing awards, and has been published in four of the DCW anthologies.

*Sidney Stevens* received an MA in journalism from the University of Michigan. Her fiction has appeared in numerous literary journals and anthologies, including *Oyster River Pages, The Woven Tale Press, The Wild Word,* and *Another Name for Darkness,* an anthology from Sans. PRESS. Her essays have been published in *Newsweek, The Dillydoun Review,* and the anthology *Nature's Healing Spirit.* She's also published hundreds of nonfiction articles and co-authored four books on natural health. See www.sidney-stevens.com.

*Chris Vannes* writes the stories that he wants to read: adventures in the hidden world all around us and the secret realms beyond our reach, tales of the futures we might build and the histories we have long forgotten. Sword fights are frequently involved. Chris is a founding board member of Dublin Creative Writers, though he and his wife have recently absconded to the mountains of New England. He plays with data for a living.

*Stephen Woodfall* is a mysterious writer, musician, and generally creative weirdo with a lifelong appreciation for speculative fiction, especially fantasy. He lives on his own in Northern California and likes movies, novels, games, and silliness. He loves sushi, but can't always afford it. Fortunately, he likes Mexican food, too, and he can usually afford that. Other items of information concerning him are closely held secrets that may or may not come to light in time.